Redemption's Road

Dawn Herbert

Redemption's Road
Copyright © 2015 by Dawn Herbert

All rights reserved. No part of this book may be used or reproduced in any manner whatsoever, including internet usage, without written permission of the author.

This is a work of fiction. Some of the characters depict actual bible figures, but their story is not necessarily this story. For factual information regarding the real people, read the Four Gospels: Matthew, Mark, Luke and John.

Scriptures have been taken directly or adapted from
THE HOLY BIBLE, NEW INTERNATIONAL VERSION®
NIV®
Copyright © 1973, 1978, 1984 by
International Bible Society ®
Used by permission.
All rights reserved worldwide.

ISBN-13: 978-0692478394
ISBN-10: 0692478396

*Dedicated to Kylie and Austin
Thank you for persevering.*

*Also dedicated to my mom and two sisters.
I thought of you in every word Jesus spoke to Mary.*

*And to Jesus, my dearest friend,
My one true love.*

ACKNOWLEDGMENTS

I would not have even considered writing a fiction had not my aunt challenged me to try. For that, thank you, Aunt Barb. You first inspired me to write when I was eight, and I have pursued that path relentlessly since then. I am grateful for your loving encouragement and the wisdom you shared on this journey. I owe you!

I would also like to expand on my dedication to my children, Kylie and Austin, who put up with torturous hours of my inattentiveness while I passionately spilled out the story God placed within. You two were troopers!

My mom and friend, Melody McDowell, put in hours of editing. Thanks, Mom, for treating this book like it mattered and giving me your wisdom in the editing process. Thanks for believing in me and urging me on. I love you!

My friend Taylor Portell also perused a very rough draft to give me ideas on how to expand on the emotional aspect of the characters. Without her wisdom, this story would be a lot less than it is. Thanks Taylor!

I would like to mention a few ladies who, in the least, invited me on an over-night women's retreat and treated me like a sister. But more than that, they all emphatically encouraged me to pick up the ball on this endeavor after a painful rejection. Jane Cook, Candy Zarcone, Mallory Zarcone, Jaclyn Rowe and Suzie Burgess, thank you so much! I am blessed to call you my friends and sisters in Christ!

A special thanks goes to a few cast members of The Great Passion Play in Eureka Springs, AR. Trent and Mallory Butler, as well as Calonese Tolbert. Thank you so much for the opportunity to shoot the cover photo on the set. What a dream come true! To Mallory and Calonese, you two took a beautiful picture!

Chapter 1

It never ceased to amaze her, this darkest hour of night. Was it bringing the dawn, or was dawn chasing it?

With a cautious, faltering breath, Mary worked her arm out from beneath the massive brute next to her. His breathing had finally slowed to a rhythmic purr, and she prayed he had enough fermented wine in him to get her out of town before he woke. With her arm free, she reached up and explored her left breast. She could feel sticky blood all over her wounded flesh, and she stifled a cry as her fingers brushed the fresh bite mark. This man was a beast. But he was also her best paying customer, and she preferred him to twenty men who paid next to nothing to have their way with her.

The slight fall to the floor reminded Mary of how reckless he had been with her. Her whole body hurt. She felt around for her dress and shawl, quickly grabbing what was under her hand when she heard him cough and stir. She wrapped the fabric around her naked body and fled into the night, tightly clutching a large bag of silver. Her weeks' wages in one night. Mary sighed gratefully. She could sleep alone a while.

Sliding in and out of the shadows, Mary made her way to her home near the edge of town. She always felt safe there, living comfortably out of sight and mind of most of the men she serviced. Mary was a lucky one. She had managed to entice the upper echelon, which was favorable both for them and herself. They bought her companionship, and she benefitted from their silent affairs. After all, Pharisees did not like to be caught with their pants down.

****

Dressed modestly with a small bag of coins tied to her wrist, Mary headed in to the market the following morning. The next day was the Sabbath and she intended to get her shopping done before the new week began. She had brought enough money to purchase fresh baked bread, fish and some new fabric. She intended to spend the afternoon making a new shawl, and hoped the merchant was selling the enchanting royal purple that had caught her eye the week before.

Winding her way through the various stands, Mary tried to keep her eyes off the men and women around her. Some of the men she recognized from the taverns she frequented. And some of the women seemed to see right through her pleasant smile and beautiful accessories. She felt weak under their tense stares and pursed lips. She noticed the way they clung to their husbands as she walked past. She was a beautiful woman walking through the market carrying her own money bag. It was both uncommon and uncomfortable.

Mary bit her lip to hide the quiver that overwhelmed her confidence and sought to betray her. Though she held her head high, her legs began to weaken under the weight of oppression around her. The stares. The whispers. The way it made her breathless with shame.

Tears stole down her cheeks and she had to lean against a table to steady herself. As her vision darkened, a familiar inner accusatory voice spit wickedly at her. "Slut. Vile waste. Wretch. Worthless."

Taunting her in rounds, the words repeated over and over until Mary buckled and fell to the ground, clutching her head with her hands. She screamed to drown them out, tearing at her hair and kicking her legs aimlessly.

Hands began to tear at her and Mary fought back hard, like a wounded wild animal. She fought until she no longer had the strength, then she lay still, curled into a fetal position with knees pulled in and her head tucked securely in between her arms.

"Ma'am, are you ok? Madame? Are you okay? Can you hear me, Madame?"

Mary blinked her eyes rapidly, searching for light and the owner of the voice. They focused on a youthful face peering into her own.

"Wha- What happened?" she stuttered, feeling lost in a sea of worried bystanders. Like a drowning victim, Mary's arms reached out desperately and she gulped the air. When it felt like the danger had passed, Mary allowed the young boy to help her to her feet, and muttered "thank you" while she steadied herself on his shoulder. Frightened and confused, Mary allowed the boy to lead her through the market stalls to a nearby cistern.

"What is happening to me?!" Mary mourned softly to herself, her eyes wide with tremulous alarm. Her face and hands were bleeding and her clothes were in shambles. She looked behind her and saw the concerned gazes of a few mixed in with the disapproving stares of many. She ducked her head in shame and hurried to distance herself from their penetrating stares.

The boy drew water for Mary, who cupped it gingerly in her hands then released it down her face and neck, pressing her palms into her skin to rub away blood and dirt. She cleaned herself and adjusted the fabric of her clothing to hide the damage. She studied the boy's face. He watched her with a mixture of fear and fascination before running off to join a small group of children playing nearby

Mary watched the market for a long time, waiting for the customers to cycle through. When enough time had passed so that all who had witnessed her episode were gone, she made her way to the fabric booth. The merchant knew her well. He stepped toward her as if they were the best of friends. In fact, he was a customer, and always treated her like his favorite meal. She smiled furtively, and he returned a wide smile.

"Mary, how are you?"

Fingering the fabric at his table, Mary squared her shoulders, taking in confidence from his demeanor. It was refreshing. "I'm well. Thank you. And you?"

They made pleasant small talk for a while, discussed several different types and shades of fabric before Mary asked about the lustrous purple fabric she had seen the last time she was in the market. He smiled slyly, disappeared behind his cart and came back with a small roll of the same fabric she had wrapped her heart around the week before. She greedily swooped it out of his hands, counted the money into his palm and turned to walk away when he grabbed her wrist.

"It's been good seeing you," he said seductively. "When can we meet again?"

Mary glanced around then slid closer to him, biting the corner of her lower lip and whispered breathily, "I guess whenever you have the time." She slipped her arm back to her hip and walked slowly away, enjoying the way he appraised her figure as she left.

Next, Mary made her way to the fruit stand and picked out a variety, added to it some vegetables, a fish, and a loaf of bread, and then walked toward the edge of town with her arms full of treasures and her heart full of joy.

She was so preoccupied with her thoughts, she failed to notice the man walking toward her until they collided. Her purchases flew in every direction as her arms flew back to soften her landing.

"Whoa!"

Embarrassed, Mary made an attempt to apologize while her eyes and hands scurried to pick up her things. Her attention was arrested, though, by the soft eyes of the man sitting opposite her. He smiled and softly laughed, the sound bubbling out in such a gentle way.

Mary had never heard such a laugh before. Her heart twisted inside her chest and she scrambled to stand up, darting after her things in an effort to escape his gaze.

The man watched her innocently without ever saying a word, as she rushed around the bend and out of sight. Mary's pace never slowed until she was standing at her own table. She spilled her load out onto the table, curled up on her bed and cried. Eventually, her exhausted body drifted into a fitful sleep. And for a while, Mary felt nothing.

Chapter 2

A rapid pounding on her door startled Mary awake. She had spent the entire Sabbath in bed, getting up in the evening to make her cherished purple shawl. The beautiful shawl now engulfed her body as she wrapped it around herself to answer the door.

The door swung wide on its hinges as Levi filled the doorway. Of course. It was the day after payday and he always came at night. He was a hopeless romantic with a less than skillful approach to women, which is what brought him often to Mary's door. She was nonjudgmental when it came to money. She also did not mind entertaining him. He was gentle and sweet with her, which was a far cry from most men she knew.

Levi walked comfortably into the room and draped his arms around Mary, one embracing her back, the other her head, as he leaned in and gently kissed her. She allowed herself the luxury of melting into his arms. Levi was an intense lover who seemed to give himself fully over to whomever held him. Mary indulged in the intimacy, even if it was temporary. He held her long, into the early morning, leaving just before dawn betrayed his confidence.

After he left, Mary exhaled heavily and began to cry. The familiar ache of disappointment and longing overwhelmed her like it always did after Levi left. His arms were so strong and comforting around her, and the way he pulled her into the curve of his body and held her without groping or engaging her in any way tricked Mary into believing there was a depth to their relationship. She always felt secure in him until this moment, when he got up and ran out. This moment left Mary feeling used and empty again. Rewrapping her shawl around herself, Mary curled up and cried herself to sleep.

****

Panting and spent, Mary ran toward the dense tree line of the wilderness. The sky was as black as pitch, like the sky before the dawn. She was breathing heavily, her heart beat almost outpacing her run as she fled from the terror behind her. She turned to see if the wolf was still chasing her and was alarmed to see that it was gaining ground.

A canopy created by dense overhanging foliage appeared ahead of her and she ran toward it, hoping to become lost among the brambles and out of reach of the monster. She ran under the canopy and realized too late her mistake; she had run straight into a well-covered lair.

Frantically, she turned to see the wolf walking menacingly toward her, and just before it pounced, its face changed grotesquely. Mary watched in horror as the wolf morphed into her father.

The dream jolted Mary from her sleep. Fear still gripped her like a vice and her hair and clothing clung to her, drenched with sweat. She bolted from the bed, gripping her shawl around her, and ran out into the early morning darkness. The quiet chatter of leaves blowing in the brisk autumn breeze was lost on Mary as she ran blindly to the brow of the cliff overlooking the sea. Tree limbs tore at her, leaving marks she had grown accustomed to overlooking. Her hair whipped across her face violently, but Mary was completely unaware of it all.

The voices inside were assaulting her, and the louder they got, the harder she ran. They spit maliciously at her, tearing her heart to shreds and violently trying to overcome her thoughts and emotions. She was certain that throwing herself into the Sea of Galilee was the only refuge from the chaotic conversations inside. Unbeknownst to her, she was a miserable host to a demonic swarm. She felt helplessly abandoned to them.

She crested the cliff and braced herself against a thin tree, allowing her lungs to recover oxygen. She stood with darkened vision, pulling in air, then melted into the dusty ground beneath her. Her body quaked as sobs overtook her determination. Crying out and moaning in agony, Mary loudly released the pain and frustration the inner war was inflicting on her.

Mary knew she was done. She had firmly decided that. How could she continue to live? Death was the only escape from the voices inside and the ravaging effects of her life. She was finally resolved to it. She was just terribly frightened by the specter of death that had chased her up the mountain.

After crawling cautiously to the edge of the cliff, Mary dug her fingers into the soft earth to anchor herself and looked over to the sea below. She heard the distant shouts of fishermen, and could see vague outlines of men along the shore, made shadows by the moonlight. They were engrossed in their work, completely unaware that a dying woman watched them from above.

Out of the corner of her eye, she noticed a man walking toward the beach. He had a slow, steady way about him, and as Mary watched him, her heartbeat began to match this new rhythm. He was a rugged man, and the calm way he walked conveyed a sense he had come just to watch the wind and the waves before the bustle of the day began.

A soothing breeze blew across Mary, and with it came a disarming sense of peace. She relaxed into a tree and watched the man at the water's edge. Her fear dissipated and a deep calm settled into her. Her breathing became natural and she became aware that the night air had dried her sweat-covered body, leaving a sticky coldness clinging to her. As uncomfortable as she suddenly was, she could not turn away to go home. She was entranced by the man on the edge of the sea. He seemed to exude all the peace and confidence Mary knew existed, but did not exist within her. She watched him for as long as he stood there, watching the eastern sunrise.

When the sun had fully exposed itself and the fishermen rowed in, the serenity was broken by the playful banter between them and the man on the shore. He interacted with ease with them, and never seemed to fall outside his element. She watched with longing until finally, she became aware of the morning heat. Rewrapping her shawl, she turned toward home with a lighter step, as her heart was no longer weighed down with fear and trepidation.

Chapter 3

There was an unusual stillness to the marketplace. Mary walked slowly through, handling trinkets and jewelry, purchasing a few and putting most back. She had more than enough money for most things she wanted, she just never really had an appetite for excess. The problem was, prostitution was a path easily fallen into, but not easily abandoned. Because it becomes a person. Mary found her worth in the arms of men, her value dictated by her own needs and desires, and sadly, her reputation surrendered the moment she succumbed to the flesh. It was a tragic irony: Mary was remarkably beautiful, and coveted by most. But wanted by none.

She felt a gentle tug on her shawl and turned to see a merchant eyeing her mischievously. She smiled politely and gave a small giggle, but then moved away to the other side of the table. He stood and walked toward her as she picked up a pair of earrings.

"You like those?" He grinned, inquisitively.

"They're very beautiful," she replied, gently placing them back where they were.

"Then very befitting for you. Please, have them." His grin became wider and Mary thought she recognized a subtle intention behind his gesture. She responded in a teasing voice, "I appreciate the gesture, but like most fine and beautiful things, the price is surely high."

He stepped in closer to Mary, and she could smell an airy musk around him. Already she knew he was not like most. He took pride in his presentation. Mary noted he was average height, and carried the paunch of a man who lived comfortably. Physically, he was not appealing to her in the least. But his subtle suggestion, mixed with a hint of expensive cologne aroused her. She felt a sudden urge within herself, a lust which became surprisingly strong when he responded, "The price is of no concern to me."

She looked around to see with whom this secret relied and was surprised that the nearby stalls and tables were empty and the merchants out of sight. The man reached out and took her hand, pulling her with him as he quickly escaped into the alley behind his table. Soon, he was pulling Mary into a small house facing the outside of town. She looked around as he began to kiss and fondle her, trying to remember to remain sensual and inviting, but becoming more and more rigid as her eyes took in the familiar sights of a family dwelling. Of a wife's delicate touch. Noticing Mary's rigidity, the man paused to search her face, but quickly dismissed her fear. "She's away at her mother's," he said nonchalantly.

As he began again to excite Mary's heart and seduce her senses, she asked, "How did you know I would come?" His lips moved down from her neck to her breasts, and she had to decipher his response, as it was mingled with the sound of her physical pleasure and his pursuit of it. It sounded like his friend, Emil, had pointed her out at the market before. While that name sounded familiar, Mary's head was clouded with other thoughts and impulses, and Emil became lost in the fray of physical sensations and breathy exclamations.

Feeling less afraid, and now more confident that she could take her time and have her way with him, Mary began to return his sensual foreplay with titillations of her own. Their voices intertwined in a duet of pleasure and surrender, and before long, the two had become entangled in bedding and clothing, and thoroughly engrossed in their sin. Their voices undulating as uniquely as their bodies, they both missed the sounds of intrusion at the door until a sharp cry pulled them rudely from their ecstasies.

A young woman stood in the doorway staring dumbfounded. In horror, Mary pulled fabric from every direction to cover herself. The man stood quickly, holding Mary's shawl in front of himself as he moved awkwardly toward his wife. The wife stood staring, her mouth agape, at Mary, as her husband began to stumble through his excuse. Tears flowed freely from her eyes. Desperately trying to avoid her miserable gaze, Mary picked through and found her clothing and clumsily got dressed. The woman began to scream at her husband again as Mary gently took her shawl from his shaky hands and walked toward the door.

A kind elderly gentleman, concerned about the sounds coming from his quiet neighbors' house, rushed in to help. Others quickly followed. Mary tried to fade into the shadows but there was no way to escape the vengeance of his wife. She turned and lunged at Mary, ripping her shawl and her dress. Fingernails clawed at Mary's face and throat, easily drawing blood and eliciting painful cries. Mary struggled for freedom against the helping hands of others who gripped the guilty parties and dragged them both out of the house.

The wife began pleading for the life of her husband, fighting to release him from the hands of his judges. Mary had no one to plead her cause, and although she had made peace with death the night before, she still fought on her own behalf. The sudden loss of control was frightening. If she were going to die, it should be in her own terms. Not at the hands of a hypocritical mob.

Mary kicked and screamed, pulling hard against the grip of the men dragging her. She cried and pleaded with them, but her pleas fell on deaf ears and cold hearts. Suddenly, pain shot through her tired body as she was thrown forcefully to the ground. She lay there heaving great sobs, waiting ...

"We found this woman in the very act of adultery. Moses said she should be stoned!"

Mary kept her face to the ground, weeping. She heard gravel grinding under the feet of her accusers as they began to pick up nearby stones. She heard their grunts and vicious snarling as they picked up the larger stones. But Mary could not understand what they were waiting for.

Tilting her head slightly upward, she saw a man near her bent down writing in the dust. He calmly lifted his eyes, and all the color drained from Mary's face. It was him. The man whose laugh had lifted her spirits and produced a sense of longing in her. The man who watched the sea, who exuded such peace and calm, Mary was better at the sight of him. This man now stood in front of her and the angry throng was demanding a sentence from him as if her fate lay exclusively in his hands. It was strange that he seemed to hold that authority. Mary was so overcome with shame, she buried her face in her arms, curled up in the dust and waited in agony.

The crowd became more violent in their accusations and questioning until the man stood. A hush fell over them when he said, "Whichever of you has never sinned should cast the first stone." Then he bent again, right next to her, and the others began to murmur among themselves. Mary could hear his gentle breath and tried to focus on the sound to keep from hearing their final judgments. She heard their voices grow louder, then she heard the sound of hurtling rocks. Fear paralyzed her and she held her breath in anticipation of the first blow. With every thudding stone, Mary felt their condemnation, but nothing ever hit her.

Finally, a gentle hand reached down to her and helped her to her feet. His eyes peered into hers and he said, "Woman, where are your accusers?"

Mary looked around, expecting to see the angry faces of men and women who now knew her terrible secret. Instead, she saw no one but him. She searched his face for answers, but he simply asked, "Has no one condemned you?"

Tears began to fall as she realized there was no one left. "No one, sir."

His gentle hands lifted her face toward his and said, "Neither do I condemn you."

As his tender words covered her shame and clothed her, his penetrating gaze exposed her down to the very marrow of her bones. Mary fell at his feet, great sobs gushing forth, releasing years of dammed up emotions. Her body heaved, her tears staining the ground at his feet. The man stood patiently as freedom and peace washed over the beautiful woman at his feet. When she had spent all her strength and emotions, he helped her to her feet again and said gently, "Go and sin no more."

Chapter 4

The days and nights began to chase one another, full of the same events, but empty of meaning. Mary did all the things she had to do without ever really engaging in them. Drawing water, doing dishes and laundry, going to the market, eating, working, sleeping. Her life was as rhythmic as it had always been, but all the sudden, meaningless.

Her men began to grumble and complain, "Where is the fun Mary? The Mary who knows how to _____?" They each filled in the blank with their own favorites, but Mary could not bring herself to relish their desires, or comply with their needs.

Rituals are strong, so the men kept coming, but none of them were happy. The money dwindled, the abuse increased, and Mary began to wonder why, with more than enough money from years of this work, she continued to entertain these men. The only man she had ever looked forward to was Levi and at some point, he stopped coming to her door. Weeks passed without him, and Mary sank farther and farther into despair, until she walked around listless.

The voices in her head became louder and louder, accusing, mocking and deriding her until she stood again on the brow of the cliff, drenched in perspiration and shaking in fear. She looked so small there. Weeks of a diminishing hunger and fitful sleep had stolen Mary's health. She was sick and tired. Weary. Desperate. Finished.

Mary stood at the very edge of the cliff and began to tease the loose rocks with her foot. Her tears had given way to an inner resolve, and she was finally mad and determined. She lifted her chin stubbornly in defiance against the cowardice and the jeering voices, stood erect and leaned forward.

At that moment, a wind blew off the surface of the sea so strongly, it nudged Mary's tiny frame back from the edge, and carried with it the sounds of rustling leaves and loud, boisterous conversations. Startled, Mary fell back to the ground, then looked past the cliff and saw an enormous throng of people heading in her direction. She panicked. Where would she go? How could she remain unnoticed?

Thousands of men and women, with their bustling children, scattered themselves out on the mountainside. They were full of laughter and joy, and their conversations floated like an amoeba above them. Panic squeezed her lungs and heart into a terrifying, rapid rhythm as Mary looked for a way through them.

Closing her eyes in an attempt to calm herself, Mary reassured herself that there had to be a way through this mess of people. But there were so many! There were no distinguishable paths around or through them.

Instead of running, Mary easily assimilated into the melee, and gravitated toward a group of women watching their children. She looked like anyone's mother, and so was left alone to her worrying and fretting over her children near the cliff. In truth, she stared vacantly out over the sea with a longing so fierce. She simply wanted to die.

"Whatcha doing?"

A curious little voice interrupted Mary's misery. A little girl, maybe three or four, sat next to her, mirroring the way she was sitting with her ankles crossed and knees drawn up to her chin. Mary smiled politely. "I'm ... watching the sea." Mary watched the chubby little face tilt toward the sea. The girl's brows wrinkled in intense concentration. "Why?" she asked finally, her eyes still glued to the horizon.

Mary laughed against her will. "Well ... I don't know," she admitted.

The little girl looked at her innocently as if studying her face, then stood and pulled Mary's arms apart. Mary's heart froze as the child wedged her tiny body in between Mary's knees and nestled herself into the gap between them. "I'm gonna watch with you," she said resolutely. She turned to face the water, leaving Mary to gape at her audacity.

Mary awkwardly put her hands on her parted knees, then moved them to the ground behind her to prop herself up, then realized there was no comfortable way to sit with this scrawny intruder in between her legs. Giving in, she picked the toddler up and crossed her legs, then set her back down in the cushion created by the fatty foldings of her lap. The little girl clasped Mary's hands in delight as she was lifted up, and although Mary quickly set her back down, her fingers remained intertwined with Mary's. She pulled Mary's arms tighter around herself and giggled.

The inner ache for security suddenly welled up in Mary, and she released it in an enormous hug, which delighted the girl further. Without another word, the two watched the water for as long as the child would sit. Then she stood abruptly. "Come with me!" she urged, pulling Mary's arm.

"Oh no," Mary said. "I think I'll just stay here. You run along, though."

"No." The girl stamped her foot and crossed her arms. "I want you to come with me." Her lower lip protruded, and she stood impatiently waiting for the effects of her pout to work its magic on Mary.

"I don't even know you," Mary said teasingly.

"I'm Gracie," she said, as if that was all Mary ever needed to know about her. Pulling Mary's arms again, she insisted, "You have to come with me!"

Reluctantly, Mary stood and brushed herself off. "Where are you going?"

"I want you to meet my momma," Gracie explained. Horrified, Mary watched Gracie skip straight into a loud group of women. "Momma! Momma!" she hollered. Mary couldn't move. She smiled weakly as Gracie led a thin woman toward her, excitedly chatting to her mother. "This is her, Momma."

"Hi," Mary said shyly.

"Hi," the woman replied.

"We were watching the sea together, Momma! Weren't we? Weren't we?" The little girl coaxed Mary anxiously.

"Yes, yes we were," Mary agreed.

"Are you staying," Gracie asked excitedly, pulling Mary toward the group as her mother laughed. Mary couldn't speak, she was so overwhelmed. Before she knew it, she was sitting in the middle of a large group of mothers with a rambunctious Gracie, who happily introduced her new friend to anyone and everyone who would listen.

The impromptu picnic lasted well into the night, and Mary warmed up to and appreciated the company. Mothers pulled her into conversations about their little ones, and because it seemed most of them just needed someone to listen, Mary was able to remain silent most of the time.

She listened to stories of children who had grown, children who had died, and children who were wrapping themselves around her legs as she smiled and nodded at their mothers. She cried with women, and found herself drawn into their arms, soaking in their grief. Mary wondered at the ease with which these women trusted her. She wondered if they would treat her the same if they knew her arms had also held their husbands, brothers, fathers, and sons.

This thought brought an intense guilt that Mary could not stifle. She excused herself under the pretense of needing to relieve herself, and vanished into the night. Her heart could not handle another moment with these people.

****

The next day, Mary went again to her mountain, but was surprised to see that the massive horde had not gone anywhere. She deftly stepped over angelic children sleeping near their mothers and fathers, and tried hard not to make much sound. But without her help, the woods began to come alive.

Mothers caressed whimpering, tired toddlers while fathers and older children ran in many different directions to relieve their morning bladders. For more than an hour, the activity seemed endless. The children cried for food while mothers opened small baskets and doled out meager portions. The older children grumbled for a while, but were silenced by a commanding voice which began to speak from somewhere up above them.

Thousands of heads turned upward, tuning in to the gentle sound of a man's voice wafting down to them. The women hushed their children and drew near to their men. Tiny families held together by a father's arms listened as stories began to form on the wind. Everyone seemed mesmerized.

Mary felt tiny hands pulling her down, so she instinctively responded to the begging girl by picking her up. Her mother was holding three other children, and so Mary sat down next to the family and listened to the wind serenade her with stories of love and victorious triumph.

Time moved quickly and without an invitation, darkness swept over them all. The voice had been drowned out hours before by the laughter and mischief of children, followed by a mass exodus of the men in the camp. They all seemed to run to higher ground, leaving mothers to tend to the flocks.

Mary had become a favored stranger among the smaller ones, who grabbed her hand and dragged her from one family to another to meet their friends and loved ones. Her heart lifted as the day wore on, until her own laughter began to spill out on to everyone around her.

Mary had forgotten what it felt like to laugh wholeheartedly, and she quickly became a contagion in the camp. Her smile and laughter touched everyone, and elicited the same response from them until the camp became flooded with joy. Mary lost herself in conversations with others, avoiding herself but maintaining their attention with life experiences that fell outside the realm of her sin. The children clung to her, and their attentions filled her with such happiness, she was sure she could not hold much more.

The darkness brought a reprieve from the hustle and bustle of little hands initiating her into surrogate motherhood. Though she adored the attention and affection, she still very much needed her space. She needed quiet time to think. To consider her place in life now. To wonder at it all. The darkness stole her companionship and gifted her with time she needed to reflect on this adventure.

As she rocked a struggling baby to sleep, holding it near her bosom, Mary reflected on the day and the things she heard. She allowed the ache for motherhood to expose itself, and buried it again by pressing her lips against the soft hair of a stranger's child. Eventually, Mary too drifted off with this baby snuggled into her motherly embrace, though her heart remained entangled in a strange mixture of reverie and guilt.

****

Mary awoke the next morning to the sounds of crying babies and tired, hungry mothers. Their conversations were not as calm and quiet as they had been, and Mary tried to make herself useful to alleviate the weight of the needs these women faced. She comforted the younger, teased the older and tried her best to distract as many as she could.

Laughter came easier the third day with these people, and Mary surrendered to the joy inside her, sharing it with those around her in any way she could.

She noticed there was a constant shifting among the people and didn't give much thought to it until he sat down near her and began to talk. "Jesus." She had heard his name whispered many times over the past two days, and finally put a face to it. It was the man of peace.

Mary allowed several boys to settle themselves in her lap, and leaned back on her hands to steady herself as they jockeyed for positions nearer and nearer her heart. Jesus kept talking and she did her best to listen to him, lost like the rest of them in the cadence of his voice and the authority he conveyed as he spoke.

Suddenly, she felt a wicked stirring in her. She abhorred him and agonizingly desired him all at once. A lusty urge began to choke her, and she pushed the children up hurriedly so she could move away. While most of them assumed she was going to relieve herself, two of them knew differently. Jesus was not unaware that she was running. And neither was Levi, who was sitting halfway up the hill, hidden by the vast number of people who had gathered to hear Jesus speak.

Mary ran down the mountainside, filled with shame at the urges rising up inside of her. Hating herself for not being strong enough to stifle them and have a normal moment with normal people. She wanted so badly to know this man, in the most innocent way, but found that she was completely unable to control her body and her mind. Her thoughts wandered down succulent paths of forbidden fruit, and Mary realized she craved this man in so many ways, both innocent and devilish.

She tried to hold on to her image of him as she had seen him with her eyes wide open, but her mind had created this alternate vision of the two of them which was altogether unholy and defiled. She ended up at the shore of Galilea, and walked into the water with a determination that was fierce and terrifying.

"Mary!"

She turned her tear-streaked face to see Levi running after her. Her heart was torn. He was chasing her. Levi. The closest thing to a lover she had ever known, and she hated him for that. Because in reality, he was nothing more than another man who was using her.

She stood defiantly, waist-deep in the water, and faced the sea to show him she was not interested. He splashed into the water behind her and grabbed for her arm. She pulled it away violently and said through clenched teeth, "Don't. Touch. Me."

Her voice was full of hatred, which shocked Levi. He stood nervously and stammered, "I'm sorry."

His apology cracked and faltered, and Mary could hear true remorse in his tone, but she was so hurt and bitter, her heart had become stone to him.

"Sorry?" She gave a sardonic snort and said, "Sorry for what? What, Levi, do you have to be sorry about? I used you too."

The pain in his face met her unforgiving gaze, and his eyes brimmed with tears. Mary's heart twisted inside her, but hatred maintained control and set her jaw firmly against him.

"I'm so sorry, Mary. For everything. I am a … a stupid man. I used you, with no regard to your heart. I used you for my own vain pleasure. I held you longer than I should have, and I confused you. And I longed for you, and sometimes thought I loved you."

His eyes and his voice dropped off at the last part, and Mary's eyes narrowed at him, hating him more fiercely than she had ever thought she might.

Levi mustered the courage to glance up at her and, although feeling her hatred penetrate his heart, he continued, "I'm sorry, Mary. That I wasn't the man I should have been. I should have never come to you in the first place. Should have never allowed myself to indulge in you. I shouldn't have …. I shouldn't have – "

"Left. You shouldn't have left. You shouldn't have stopped coming to me like I was common refuse. I expected it from everyone else. I expected their hatred and rejection. But you, Levi … in some strange way, you and I were more intimately connected. I felt in the least you were my friend. I never expected you to disappear. To altogether throw me away without ever seeing me again in some capacity."

She set the stone resolutely in place when she added through clenched teeth, "I didn't expect to ever hate you as much as I do right now."

Levi could see that she really did hate him. The truth was boiling behind her golden eyes. His heart broke.

"Mary, I didn't stop coming over because I was done with you. It isn't what you think. I stopped be –"

"I don't care," she said quietly. "I don't care why you stopped. Just go away."

She walked past him back to the shore, muffling her heart's cry. Levi followed her, and when she slumped to the sand, her body wracked with emotion, he knelt next to her and tried to explain.

"I stopped coming, Mary, because I met Jesus. And I realized I didn't want to hurt or use you anymore. You are worth more than I or anyone else has ever paid you, Mary. And you deserve to know that. And I wanted to tell you that from the bottom of my heart, I am sorry for treating you like anything less than a beautiful woman worthy of my utmost honor and respect."

Mary cried harder and forcefully pushed away Levi's attempts to hold and comfort her. "No!" she screamed. "Don't touch me!"

Levi hurt for her. He wanted to comfort her, but he wrestled with the fact that she did not want him to.

Mary wept for what seemed to Levi like an eternity. He cautiously knelt next to her, and wrapped her in his arms again. This time, she did not resist. He held her as she cried, until an awkward awareness of how it might look to others began to pull him to his feet.

Mary clutched his arm tightly, desperately clinging to the comfort of his embrace and dragging his attention back to the woman he had devastated.

"Please, Levi. Please! Take me to him. I must meet this man, Jesus."

Chapter 5

When Mary and Levi reached the place they had last seen Jesus, the people were scattered everywhere, talking excitedly. Everyone was passing around and devouring fish and bread, and telling of how Jesus had taken a few meager pieces of each and miraculously created this feast for all of them.

Mary looked around, absorbing the delight of the people around her and allowing her heart to roam free in their jubilation. She sat beside an older girl, who handed her some bread, and they soon delved easily into conversation.

Levi stood near her, scanning the crowd for Jesus. His voice began to drift down to them, quieting the multitude, and Levi could see that he would be impossible to get to for a while. He smiled reassuringly at Mary and moved to sit with the men who had gathered nearby to eat.

The conversations lasted well into the night. Once again, Mary found herself soothing sleepy babies. Her heart was full of love for this group of strangers, and her need for Jesus was intensified by the needs of the people around her. It was as if there was a harmonious burning desire among them all for more of him.

****

Mary awoke the next morning to murmuring in the camp. She listened intently and overheard that Jesus had left during the night. Families began to wake and leave, some hurrying away to town and others taking their time, hiking further up the mountain.

A small troupe gathered on the beach, wondering where he might have gone. There was a boat missing along the shore, and they assumed that Jesus had left for Capernaum. Some of the men began to prepare a boat to follow, and without asking, many others climbed into the boat to go. Mary climbed in too. It was as if in one accord, they had decided to follow him.

Mary sat in the boat next to a woman holding a newborn baby. "Your child is a boy or a girl?" she asked the proud mother.

"A girl," the mother replied with a sweet, loving smile. The women both looked at the calm, sleeping baby, adoring the look of content on her face.

"She can't be very old," Mary mused.

"No," the mother cooed softly. "Just a few months."

"Oh goodness! And now, already, you are here, pursuing Jesus?!"

"Oh yes! Jesus has made everything about my life right. I cannot lose sight of him. Where would I be without him?!"

The look of genuine affection so affected Mary that tears came to her eyes. Reaching out to the woman, she pleaded, "Please, tell me, what has he done?"

The woman gestured to Mary as if she should take the baby. Mary was more than obliging. The new mother situated herself to become more comfortable, and then looked off into the distance as if seeing her memories as she spoke.

"I was at the well. It was the middle part of the day, and very hot." Her face changed to show the pain of remembering, and Mary was captivated by the anticipation she felt.

"You may wonder why I was at the well at that time of day. After all, most women draw water early in the morning to avoid the heat. I drew in midday to avoid the women."

She laughed a gentle laugh, reassuring Mary that this story, though exposing her shame, was as worth telling as it was listening to.

"A man came and sat on the edge of the well right next to me and asked me for a drink. I looked him over and scoffed, 'You are a Jew, and I am a Samaritan. How can you ask me for a drink?' Then I turned away from him and kept drawing up my own supply. But he said, 'If you knew the gift of God and who it is that asks you for a drink, you would have asked him and he would have given you living water.'"

Her facial expressions conveyed her emotions of that day, and Mary watched and listened eagerly, becoming lost in the story as the woman became more and more animated.

"I looked at him like he was crazy! He had nothing to draw with, and the well was deep! And I told him so! I said, 'Are you greater than our father, Jacob, who gave us this well, and drank from it himself?'

"All the while I was talking, his calm eyes watched me, and never betrayed an emotion. His reply amused me even more. He said, 'Everyone who drinks of this water will be thirsty again, but whoever drinks the water I give them will never thirst. Indeed, the water I give them will become in them a spring of water welling up to eternal life.'

"I laughed at him at that. I said mockingly, 'Oh sir, give me this water so I won't get thirsty and have to keep coming here to draw water.' But his next statement knocked the smile right off my face. He said, 'Go, call your husband and come back.' I looked at him nervously and admitted, 'I have no husband.'" Her voice dropped low, and she said it as if still living in the nakedness of that moment. She went on.

"He was so kind when he said to me, 'You are right when you say you have no husband. The fact is, you have had five husbands, and the man you have now is not your husband.' I felt completely exposed to him, and full of shame. And somewhat in awe of him. 'Sir, I can see you are a prophet. I know the Messiah, called Christ, is coming.'

"His face warmed with a wide smile as he said, 'I, the one speaking to you, am he.' And I could see it. It was like my eyes were opened for the very first time and I was looking into the face of my savior!

"His friends came to him then and tore his attention from me, so I ran to town. I ran harder and faster than I had ever run before and I shouted at the top of my lungs that I had met the Messiah. I hadn't talked to most of those people in years. I hadn't been out in public in years! But they had to know! I told them all 'He told me everything I ever did!'

"At that, people began to run toward Jacob's well. I ran to find my man, and I told him too. He was so skeptical, but I dragged him toward the well until he finally relented and walked with me. When we got there, Jesus was teaching the whole town wonderful things we'd never heard before.

"It was so weird. We could feel in our hearts that everything he was saying was true. For hours, we sat listening to him. Then my husband," she looked at a young man who was standing near the front of the boat and smiled lovingly, 'who of course, was not my husband yet ... he invited Jesus to our house. And he came! He came and stayed with us three days! Our children played all over him and his friends. We talked more than we slept. And we were so affected by him, we decided to commit our hearts to him.

"Also," she said, with a twinkle in her eye, "to one another." She grinned so wide with joy and squealed, "He married me! And now we have this beautiful baby as a symbol of our love before God. I mean, our other children are of course, wonderful blessings and gifts. But this child," she gently lifted the baby from Mary's arms and pulled her in close to her heart. "She is a gift honoring our commitment."

The woman looked at Mary with tears in her eyes and said, "This baby is the first baby I have had within a covenant marriage."

She reached out for Mary's hand and pressed it hard. "This baby is my fifth. And for the first time in my life, I am not overwhelmed or fearful of being her mother. For the first time in my life, I am confident in the man I married that he will be here every day for the rest of my life and help me raise my children in the fear and admonishment of God. It's so wonderful!"

Mary smiled at the woman, who sat smiling at her husband as he helped pull the boat onto the shore. They had reached Capernaum.

Chapter 6

Peering into the distance, Mary could see a small fire and people scattered around it. Leaving the others to deal with the boat, she walked toward the fire. There was just a small group of men there, sleeping in the sand.

After tending to the fire, Mary sat down in the sand near the man she now knew was Jesus and watched him sleep. His chest rose and fell in that soft rhythm that drew her into a calmness she always experienced around him. She watched him contentedly for a while without making a sound, until the group from the boat caught up to her.

The natural noise that accompanied them roused the sleeping men. Mary noticed that Levi was there also. He had been sleeping on his stomach at the far outer edge of the group.

She turned back to see Jesus walking away from the group, but restrained a deep-seated urge to follow him. She wanted so badly to be alone with him. To talk to him one-on-one. There were things she needed to ask him, and things she wanted to hear for herself. But she knew she shouldn't seek to be alone with him yet. He didn't even know her. And she was sure Levi would expose her shame to these people she had grown to love. They did not know her well enough to do anything but love her back. She was sure that if they knew anything about her, they would all hate and desert her too. And she could not bear that. So she stayed near the fire and listened to others share their stories of healing and deliverance by this man called Jesus.

Across from Mary sat a man who excitedly shared that he had been a leper until that morning. There was another man who claimed to have been demon-possessed until Jesus came to him. He enthusiastically shared his life's story of increasing torment which Mary found frighteningly similar to her own past. A rapidly fading health and a spiraling sanity. Dark nights filled with broken memories. Lapses of time he could not recall, and accusations he could not admit or deny. Pieces of his life were missing! And then he met Jesus.

When he revealed that at first, he hated Jesus fiercely, Mary's heart broke. But then he shared of the kind, calmness of Jesus that stilled the man's racing thoughts, drew him out of his inner darkness, and set him free. Literally, set him free! Those around him nodded their heads as if they had witnessed his story of demons leaving him. His story astonished and amazed Mary.

One after another, for hours, they shared. And the whole time, Jesus was gone. Mary finally went to Levi and inquired anxiously, "Is he coming back, Levi?"

The need in her was growing with each tale of victory she encountered. Noticing a wild, uneasy look in her eyes, Levi's heart twisted in anguish.

"Mary, are you okay"

"I need him, Levi. I need ... whatever it is that has healed and restored these people." Her voice broke. "I'm dying, Levi. I've been dying for as long as I can remember. And you all seem so ... alive. You're happy, and you laugh, and the laughter never leaves your eyes. I laugh but inside, I am still dying."

She grabbed his arm forcefully and said, "I need to be able to breathe. I need to be able to feel. I need him! Don't you see?!"

Tears streamed down her face and Levi could see her desperation. Yes, she needed him. As Levi had once needed him.

Mary noticed his eyes struggle between a distant pain and a present joy. She searched his face and implored, "Tell me. Tell me what it was like for you. Please!"

Levi stood and motioned for her to follow. He led her away from the group and sat on a rock near the water. Mary settled beside him and looked out over the sea.

"You know, Mary, that I was a tax collector."

"Was?"

"Yes, was. I will get to that. Please, let me just start there. I was sitting at the booth one day, with a long line of angry men waiting for their turn to speak to me. Each man held his tax papers in his fist, shouting at me to explain the charges I had written for them. I don't know what brought them all at once to me."

He lowered his head in shame and continued. "I had been overcharging all of them for years. Rome takes so much, and I take the rest. That's my duty as a tax collector. That's my livelihood. Rome doesn't pay me. I make my own way. I take Caesars and mine."

He talked as if defending himself, but she knew he was feeling the guilt of his past.

"For whatever reason, they all converged on me at one time, and I didn't have an excuse. For the first time in my life, I was looking for a reason and drawing a blank. These men, their faces were red and their eyes were full of fury and hatred. Then someone shoved me and another hit me, and I fell back into the dust. I expected all of them to beat me to a bloody pulp. Mary, I expected to die."

The fear in his eyes was convincing. Mary nodded to urge him to continue.

"At that moment, this man came up through the crowd and everyone got quiet. He came up to me and asked me what we were having for dinner. I looked at him like he'd lost his mind! He just helped me up and laughed and said, 'You must have forgotten I was coming!' Then he hit my shoulder hard as if we were the best of friends and said, 'You said six, right? I'll see you then.'

"While the men around me stood dumbstruck, I quickly gathered my things and left. Sure enough, this guy showed up at my house at six that evening with food and wine. Which was a good thing, because I can't cook!"

His attempt at a joke fell flat. Mary was so eager to hear the rest, she couldn't register the humor in his voice.

Levi's face grew serious again as he continued telling her about the evening with Jesus.

"It was just he and I at first. He introduced himself, laid out the food and while he poured us wine, asked me what had been going on when he first came up to me that afternoon. I felt like I was in some sort of parallel universe. This man was acting like we had known each other forever, and I had only just heard of him and seen him from a distance. But I was so comfortable despite all these facts that I told him. Everything. I told him about my job, and how I'd been manipulating the system to cheat families out of money. How I had made my living entirely from extortion."

Dropping his head into his hands, Levi began to sob. Mary reached out to him, placing a hand on his shuddering shoulder, and watched him cry. Looking back toward the fire, she noticed that Jesus had returned.

She shook Levi and pointed toward the fire. He quickly wiped his eyes and stood with her. Making their way back to the gathering, they stood behind the group to listen to Jesus, who was speaking as they came.

"...and you shall know the truth and the truth will set you free."

He looked up and met Mary's eyes as he said, "And whom the Son sets free is free indeed."

Mary locked into his gaze, as Jesus delved into the epicenter of her soul. She could feel an emotional storm growing rapidly inside her. Hatred rose up into her throat and choked her as something of an inner war began. Mary struggled to maintain eye contact with him.

His eyes remained on her, and her breathing became rapid and shallow. She felt her jaw line tense and saliva flooded her mouth. Gathering it up with her tongue, she spit maliciously at Jesus. The others drew back with alarm. Levi moved toward Mary, but stopped when he saw Jesus stay him with a wave of his hand.

Mary's voice became low and guttural and she hissed, "What do you want with me?"

Her voice became louder, more aggressive as she repeated, "What do you want with me?"

Those around them backed away in fear as she moved menacingly toward the fire, closer to Jesus. Then she shouted, "What do you want with us?" and lunged toward him.

He stood, and Mary fell back as if she had hit a brick wall. Jesus commanded, "Silence!"

Everything in the world around them became still. Mary lay on the ground looking up at him, her face distorted in what appeared to be both fear and pain. Jesus pointed his finger toward the southern sky and spoke low and calm, "Demons, go."

Horrible screams filled the air, and Mary's body convulsed as a dark vaporous thing shot out of her mouth and seemed to split apart as it flew skyward. Levi could see seven distinct pieces of the demonic cloud rush into oblivion. He watched as Jesus knelt beside Mary and, placing a hand gently on her said, "You are free."

Mary's limp, seeming lifeless body began to stir. She weakly pushed herself up to a sitting position and looked into the face of Jesus. The spit was still there, on his face, but he didn't seem to notice. His eyes were on her, and she could feel a warmth coming from him that engulfed her and made her feel as if she was wrapped in a soft fur blanket.

She held his gaze, feeling vulnerable but completely unafraid. Hugging herself with one arm, she hesitantly reached up with the other and wiped the spit from his face. Then she smiled and looked away.

The beach exploded with excited conversation, and Mary was swept up in the jubilation of her own story. The men and women around her spoke over and under each other trying to put the pieces together for Mary. Her own story. She felt like her head was spinning!

Her attention flitted here and there trying to fully comprehend the events of the past few minutes. Re-enactments of Mary's testimony scattered out across the beach, and she sat there watching in wonder at it all.

Levi sat down next to her, and she smiled over her shoulder at him. Then her eyes caught the sight of Jesus walking away down the beach alone. But this time, peace flooded her as she knew in her heart he would be back.

Chapter 7

Mary sat quietly, still overwhelmed with new emotions. She was happy, and her heart felt so light. The people had gathered around the fire and were still talking animatedly about deliverances and the differences in themselves and others since Jesus had come.

Food came from every direction and the group shared willingly with one another. Everyone ate and had their fill, and then the women gathered to one side of the campfire, and men to the other, and they all lay down to sleep.

Mary pulled her shawl around her body and lay her head on her arm. Still too excited to sleep, she lay there thinking about the day and about Jesus. He still had not returned to the group, but she was full of a calm expectation that assured her she would see him again. She had to. There was so much she needed to say to him.

Recognizing a woman lying near her, Mary reached out to touch her side. The woman turned, the baby snuggled into her bosom, and smiled sweetly at Mary. Mary smiled back.

"Please, can you tell me again how it happened?"

It took a few seconds for the woman to reposition herself to keep her sleeping child comfortable and also face Mary, but soon, she was recounting every detail of Mary's deliverance in hushed excitement. Mary's serene smile remained even as she plunged into a deep, peaceful sleep.

****

Mary woke at daybreak. The moon was full, and the beach well lit, so she stood and silently walked away from the group to the water's edge. Her steps were slow, reflecting the steadiness in her heart and mind. There was a tranquility about Mary that showed on the outside, mirroring the inside. It was a newness she was already in love with. A harmony reposed in the place chaos had always been. Her emotions, once as turbulent as a stormy sea, were placid.

She walked alone along the water's edge, attuning herself to the cadence of the waves and wind intermingling with sharp staccato cries of birds. The sound of dawn approaching was a beautiful symphony Mary loved to hear. This was her favorite part of day. She breathed deeply, filling herself with the soothing calm of morning. Closing her eyes, she inhaled again, long and slow as smile crept into her soul.

She was pulled abruptly from her meditations by the rude sound of sloshing feet. Opening her eyes she recognized a man who'd been with the group walking proudly toward her. He smiled conspiratorially and Mary hugged herself and turned away, hoping he would take the hint and leave. Instead, he walked right up to her and leaned in uncomfortably close.

"Hey there. Mary, is it?"

Mary turned toward him, her arms still crossed, and tried to remain pleasant although inwardly, she was uncomfortable and a bit frightened by him. "Yes. And you are?"

"Judas," he said, casting a nervous glance over his shoulder as his hand reached out and softly brushed her upper thigh.

Mary stepped away, astonished at his brazenness. "Judas. I'm not interested."

Judas held up a bag and shook it for affect. The sound of coins meant to tempt Mary fell on deaf ears. She genuinely wasn't interested. Whatever had happened earlier, whatever demonic stronghold had been broken, Mary now found that she was completely repulsed by Judas' attempt to allure her.

Turning away, Mary began to walk further along the beach, but Judas took a long step and stayed in stride with her. Smiling to mask an anger coming over him, he gruffly pulled Mary to him, his arm anchored around her waist. He kissed her forcefully, and pulled her tightly into him. She could feel a pulsing hardness pushed into her lower abdomen, and Judas towered over her menacingly. "I am," he hissed.

Mary shoved him, straining to pull herself away from him, but his grip on her was strong. He fell onto her, and she suddenly felt trapped beneath the weight and strength of a hundred men. She had never experienced such physical strength, and she struggled against the paralyzing fear that threatened to overcome her.

Judas tried again to kiss her, and she shoved her face into his. The pain shocked them both, and he let go of her wrist and hit her hard in the face.

Though she yelped at the pain, she reflexively reached under him and squeezed his groin hard. His face contorted violently in reaction, and he folded up in pain on top of her.

The adrenaline coursing through her helped her shove him over onto the beach. Mary stood weakly and fled up the beach toward the fading coals of the fire. She was breathing heavy and shaking violently, full of fear and anger. With nowhere else to go, she curled her quaking body up near her sleeping friend and muffled her sobs with her beautiful purple shawl. Eventually, sheer exhaustion took over, and carried Mary back into a weary, heavy sleep.

Chapter 8

A gentle tug of her shoulder startled Mary awake. She rolled over, at first alarmed, to see who was touching her. The fear she felt remembering her earlier altercation with Judas melted away when she looked up into the face of Jesus.

She quickly sat up and pulled her shawl around her shoulders as if to protect herself from him. She glanced around to see others in various activities; some tending to loved ones, some heading off into the woods, and still others burrowed deeply into dreams they still had not awaken from.

Jesus offered her his hand and gently helped her to her feet. His piercing eyes met hers. "Come, Mary. Walk with me."

As if entranced, Mary stepped lithely through the scattered bodies of heavy sleepers, and followed Jesus to the lake shore.

Bending down, Jesus picked up a rock, turned it over in his hands as if studying it, and then skipped it across the surface of the water. Mary could see a deep concentration on his face, and because she was near him at his own invitation, she decided to wait until he spoke to break the silence between them.

She appreciated his invitation to walk with him, and she was desperate to talk to him. There was so much she wanted to say. So many things she wanted to ask. But for the moment, it was enough to be near him.

Mary watched him as he continued to pick up objects and hurl them into the lake. Rocks, sticks, clumps of dirt. He was making a sport of trying to best the distance each throw succeeded while Mary simply enjoyed the fact that Jesus seemed ... normal.

His feet were bare and sandy from the beach, his clothing dirty from days sleeping on the ground, and his hair was disheveled and slightly greasy. He smelled like the sand and the sea, the earth and his own natural musk. She had definitely smelled worse.

He seemed so comfortable. Comfortable in the silence between them. Comfortable despite her obvious scrutiny. Comfortable enough to laugh at himself when he accidently loosed a rock behind himself on the backswing.

His laughter pulled Mary out of her contemplation, and she giggled in response to his bubbly laugh. It was a beautiful sound that induced a melodic, contagious joy between them. Enticed by it, Mary and Jesus laughed and smiled at each other for a good while, without either feeling self-conscious. Finally, Jesus stopped and looked at Mary. Her smile reached up to her eyes and touched the new sparkle there.

"You are very beautiful, Mary."

He said it like it was a fact. Not like most men, who said it flirtatiously or seductively. He said it like she just needed to hear it. And she realized how much she did need to hear it. Just like that. Like it was a fact.

Jesus did not reach out to touch her, or move toward her in any way. He simply stood there with his hands hanging by his sides looking into her eyes. There was no intention, no implications. Mary felt something awaken in her. An innocence, reflecting the innocence of Christ.

"Thank you."

She held his gaze, unable to look away. This was the first time in her life she actually felt beautiful. Not lusty, not wanted. Just beautiful.

Jesus smiled, turned and continued walking. Mary walked gracefully beside him, keeping in step with his slow, steady pace.

Further along, they came to a cluster of rocks and Jesus perched on one, gesturing for Mary to sit on another. She did, turning her face to catch the breeze off the water and momentarily escape his penetrating gaze. Pulling her shawl tighter around her shoulders, Mary hugged her knees for comfort.

Mary had never been around a man in such an innocent, pure way. She didn't know how to have a conversation devoid of subtle hints and vulgar intentions hidden beneath the surface. She didn't know how far to let his compliment into her heart, although she was strongly tempted to believe him.

All the while, Jesus watched with fascination, knowing that Mary was struggling through all she knew from her past trying to make sense of him.

"Mary."

She turned to look at him, and sighed heavily.

"What is it, Mary, that you wanted to talk about?"

Mary dropped her eyes to the ground and shifted nervously, feeling very exposed. He knew. He knew she needed to talk to him, and he had invited her to walk with him so she could. She searched for the best way to begin. So many thoughts and questions raced through her mind.

"Who are you?" She blurted out, and immediately felt foolish as he burst out a loud laugh in response.

Jesus shifted on the rock to turn toward her and said, "I am ... who I am." He shrugged nonchalantly. "I guess as to who that is, you will come to decide for yourself. For now, let's just say I am. Jesus."

He said this last part with a small smile, and Mary felt his smile reach into her heart and pull out the next question. She would have stopped it if she could, but she was being drawn with cords of his kindness, and it spilled out from the deep recesses of her soul, "Who am I?"

The sudden feeling of nakedness startled Mary so much, she began to cry. She wished at once she could take the question back. She wished she had not revealed her inner need so quickly to this familiar stranger. But she felt so secure, she had let her guard down and her heart was demanding to know. Something in her pleaded with him, sure that he somehow knew the answer.

She covered her face and wept, years of pent-up anxiety and pain pouring out of her. It felt like a cleansing, and Jesus remained a silent observer. He was unobtrusive, which was such a relief to Mary. She needed this. She allowed herself to cry until her body was emptied. Then she wiped her eyes, but kept them focused on the crevice between her rock and his, peering into it as if looking for a lost treasure.

She was unwilling to look up at him, but Jesus maintained his fixed gaze on her until finally, he said, "Who are you, Mary?"

Mary looked up. Jesus was looking at her, and she felt as if he was peering into the center of her heart. Like a child beckoned to come clean, Mary struggled with an inner compulsion to spill everything out before him. She shivered in reaction to the memory of her childhood: the hunger, the loneliness. Fears that haunted her every waking minute until finally, they became a reality. Her father seeking womanly comfort from her frail girlish body.

She wrestled to hold back all the memories whose reality had long since caused her to die inside. She thought about the men who paid her father for her favors. And then after his passing, who simply continued to pay her. Mary had accumulated vast amounts of money selling her emptiness.

Her voice faltered as she grappled for the words, vacillating between fierce anger, bitterness, remorse, pain, and a tormented whisper, until finally, "I ...I'm not sure."

"Look at me, Mary." His voice was gentle, yet commanding.

Facing him, Mary steeled herself to meet his eyes.

"Who are you?"

He said it again, and Mary knew he was again drawing something out of her. She furrowed her brow in intense concentration, trying to understand the emotions going through her and the thoughts racing through her mind. She tried to capture a coherent thought so she could answer him, but there was just too much going through her. Finally, she gave up.

"I don't even know."

Once again, she looked out across the sea, feeling empty and defeated. She heard Jesus moving, and did not blame him for walking away. She had shared nothing with him. Unwilling to watch him go, she kept her face defiantly toward the water.

Jesus placed his hand delicately on her shoulder and said, "I know you, Mary." She looked up into his face and saw a deep compassion there. He smiled and took her hand. Mary slid off the rock and together they began to walk back toward the others.

In a quiet, squeaky voice, Mary said, "Please tell me, then, who am I?"

"In time, I will."

Chapter 9

Jesus and Mary returned to find that the others had prepared the boat to sail back to Bethsaida. Mary was relieved to be heading home. Her clothes were worn out from days of wear, her body hurt from the rough nights on the ground, and she needed the sanctuary of home to process the last few days of her life.

Climbing into the boat, Mary found a place with the women to sit. She noticed that Judas was still on the shore, and that was a great comfort to her.

The woman next to her began talking in her direction, and Mary quickly became engrossed in conversation. She felt the boat shove off, but kept her attention fastened to the woman beside her. She was beginning to enjoy the company of these women, and did not want to offend her by not acknowledging the conversation.

They had been on the sea quite some time before Mary's attention was released to wander and she realized that Jesus was not on the boat either. Nor was Levi.

Mary became inwardly frantic and disappointed. She no longer felt confident about going home. Instead, she felt abandoned to a world that she wanted desperately to escape.

She attempted to maintain focus on the conversations around her, but her mind was miles away, searching the far off coast of Capernaum for any sign of where Jesus may have went. How did she not notice he was gone? How could she face her old life without his reassurance and strength?

She felt foolish, because in reality, she hardly knew Jesus. Yet when she was with him, she felt like she had known him forever. Moreover, she felt safe with him. And alive. And okay.

Mary was despondent the rest of the way home, and the women found her unengaging. Eventually, the conversations drifted further away from her ears and the others huddled inward to break the wind as much as possible. Mary faced it, allowing the wind and water to have its way with her. She was hardly aware of it; her mind was on Jesus. Somehow, she had to get back to him

****

Her home was quiet and strangely uninviting. After spending several days with multitudes of people, with continuous conversations and boisterous children playing nearby all day, Mary could hardly bear the silence of her house. Gathering clean clothes, she headed to the river to bathe, hoping there would be women and children nearby she could fall in with. The well-worn path was vacant, as was the beach.

Mary went to a small cove and quickly bathed and redressed. She gathered her things and set off toward home. When she got there, she was surprised by a man peering into her front door.

"Can I help you?" She asked, quickly working the bundle of dirty clothing in her hands so that it was small and unassuming. She shifted it to one hand and tousled her wet hair with the other. Looking into the man's eyes, Mary tried to portray all the confidence in the world to hide her discomfort and distrust, and prayed she fooled him.

"I'm looking for Mary. I was told she lived here, and I've come ... Do you know her."

His voice was equally confident, and Mary couldn't help but notice what a huge man he was. His arms bulged out of his sleeves, and his lower body reminded her of a tree. Stocky and unmoving.

Suddenly, she hated her solitude. She hated how far from town she lived, how isolated she had made herself to hide her shame. She prayed this man had some level of integrity.

"The Mary you are looking for no longer lives here."

She glided past him and walked into the house, hoping she had just dismissed him. His shadow covered the table she placed her things on, and his body still filled the doorway, only now, it was blocking her entrance completely. Mary squared her shoulders, silently prayed and turned to face him.

The man was looking her over as if she were a high-priced steak. He licked his lips in a seductive way Mary had seen too many times before.

"What about you?" he said.

"I'm sorry, sir, I'm not sure why you came but I told you, the woman you are looking for no longer lives here."

Mary reached for the door to close it, but the man blocked it with his foot. A chill crept up her spine and sent a shiver down her body.

"I heard you. But you look just like the woman I heard tell about, and I came with quite the appetite."

As he spoke, he inched his way into the room. Mary's heart was pierced by the reality of what was happening. She did her best to hide her trembling, but she was quaking inside with fear. It was more than not wanting to be taken without her consent. Of course, she hated that. It had happened to her so many times, though, she was used to that loss of control.

But after spending time with Jesus, she had made up her mind to keep herself from promiscuous, unemotional sex. *"Go and sin no more,"* he has said. And Mary intended to. Yet here was a man who was threatening to take that from her. And she had no escape.

Mary stumbled over her words as she tried to politely to dismiss him, and then less politely tried to get around him. The gigantic stranger stepped directly in front of her and grabbed her waist very gruffly.

Kicking and screaming, Mary fought hard to escape, but he held her as if she were a child in a tantrum. While she punched, scratched and bit him in every place unlucky enough to come within her limited reach, he tore at her clothing until she was fighting naked, tears streaming down her face.

He pushed her into the floor and straddled her squirming body with his massive trunk on top of her thighs and his legs squeezed uncomfortably tight around her legs. His right hand held both of her wrists together above her head and he used his left arm to position himself. His legs loosened around hers, but not enough for her to fight with them. Just enough for him to penetrate her.

He kept a vise-like grip on her wrists, and with his free hand, fondled her breasts while he took her.

Mary screamed until she was hoarse, then just stopped. Stopped screaming, stopped fighting, stopped caring. She let him have his way, listening to his breath quicken then subside with release, felt him fill her.

He thrust a few more times, grunting with pleasure, then lowered himself to rest on top of her. His sweat trickled down her neck, and the feeling of it made Mary sick. Turning her head to the side, Mary vomited.

The man pushed himself up, startled and disgusted. He drew back his left hand and backhanded her with such strength, Mary barely had time to register the pain before she blacked out.

A sharp pain brought Mary back to. She had been moved to her bed, and the man was again on top of her, panting and grunting. Mary could feel the sheets beneath her and her hands were free. Her right arm was thrown out to the side, her fingers falling off the edge of the bed. Her left arm was positioned up, her hand laying softly just over her head.

He was so distracted by his business, he was not aware that she was awake. Looking around frantically, Mary tried to formulate a plan to escape him, but quickly realized there was no way out of this hellish nightmare. She was sure she was not safe as long as he was conscious. She resigned herself to waiting him out, and prayed he would eventually get sick of her inactivity or wear himself out on her. Maybe then he would leave.

Mary endured what seemed like an eternity of interrupted abuse. Her abuser would stop long enough to breathe in the fullness of sexual pleasure, then he was at it again. He no longer even tried to engage her. He didn't speak. He didn't ask her permission. He just acted like she was his, and he took her over and over, even though she refused to play along with him.

Sometime in the night, he finished again, dropped his weight on her and panted for several painstaking minutes, then got up and walked out without a backward glance.

Mary lay there, afraid to move. Afraid to believe he was really gone, lest he come back in and destroy her hope. Her eyes were wide, watching the door.

She lay that way for another hour, and when she was sure he was not coming back, she tried to sit up on the edge of her bed. Pain shot through her body. Groaning, Mary slowly curled into a fetal position and bawled. He had used her so brutally, she was torn and in intense pain.

Finally, an angry, fierce determination overtook her. Ignoring the pain, she stood on shaky legs and shuffled to the table where she grabbed a garden spade. Then she walked outside and around her house to her garden in the back.

It was a flower garden. Mary spent much of her time in her garden, pulling weeds and coaxing things to grow. She also buried her secrets there. Each flower was planted over a bag of money. It was a strange way to keep her money, but thus far, this system had ensured she never got robbed. She did not keep any money in the house because she had seen men rummage through her things looking. Every one of them had left disappointed that they couldn't take more from her. She felt a personal victory every time.

Mary fell with a roaring sob into the middle of her garden, and began to tear at the flowers. Pulling whole flowers out of the ground, she stabbed her spade forcefully into the dirt and dug up money.

Screaming in anger, Mary clenched her teeth and kept pulling up and digging until her garden was completely decimated. Bags of coins were everywhere. More than a hundred of them, cinched tightly and flung carelessly around the yard. The full moon shown on her spoils, and Mary in her nakedness, lying prostrate in what used to be a beautiful garden, clutched the dirt and poured out her broken heart to the night.

The destruction around her was indicative of the destruction within. One night had turned the beautiful promise of Mary's life into a nightmare she lived every day after. Before her mother's death, Mary was a little girl blossoming under the love and affection of her parents. She was radiant with joy, with a smile that could light up any room. Now ... now she was a wreck. Completely destroyed by the evil inclinations of mankind that had become her enemy.

When she had no more tears to spend, Mary picked herself up from the beautiful ruins of her garden and slowly made her way inside. Wearily, she lay on her bed and watched for the dawn through the door she left open. Her eyes watched the sky while her heart cried out for Jesus.

Chapter 10

Several days later, a very tired, weak Mary roused herself to get dressed. She walked outside and to her backyard where she slowly scooped up bags of money. Placing them into her shawl until it was heavy, she carried them inside.

After a few trips, Mary's table was covered in small bags, some adorned, some plain. All holding gold and silver coins. She emptied each of them into a clay vase, and when it was full, she filled a second, then a third, fourth and fifth. Finally, she was finished. Her life's savings filled five vases. Mary exhaled her relief; she would never have to work again. She was done.

She pushed the vases far beneath her bed and then walked back down the path to the cove to wash her bruised, dirty body. When she was clean, she reversed course and walked all the way to town.

In the market, she bought two large satchels, a few things to pull her hair back with, and several new undergarments and dresses. She was halfway home with her things when she noticed a young woman she had met on the mountainside. Mary smiled and tried to wave, but her hands were full and she dropped several things instead. The woman was already walking toward her, and they both laughed, then stooped to pick up Mary's belongings.

"How are you, Mary?" the other woman asked, holding out Mary's things to her. Quickly realizing Mary had no more hands to hold them with, she held them herself and began to walk in the direction Mary was going.

"I'm ... I'm sorry, I recognize your face, but I just can't seem to recall your name ..."

The woman laughed heartily and said, "Actually, it's Martha. My sister's name is Mary. That's how I remembered yours."

Mary smiled self-consciously. "Martha. Thank you for remembering me. How are you?"

"I'm great! How are you?"

Martha's smile was charming, and disarming, and soon, Mary had forgotten for a time the prison her life had become and was enjoying the pleasant company of another human being again. They talked all the way back to Mary's house, and before she really thought it through, Mary had invited her new friend inside.

Money sacks were thrown everywhere, and her bed was in shambles. But Martha was kind enough to not acknowledge the mess, which made Mary more determined to like this woman.

Mary shared her lunch, and the two talked for a while before Martha forgot herself enough to ask Mary what she had been up to, as if they were long-lost friends.

Thrown completely off guard, Mary hesitated, started to speak and then stopped, backtracked, fidgeted uncomfortably then said, "I'm sorry, I have some things I need to get done."

Standing abruptly, Mary began to clear the table. Realizing she had been dismissed, Martha stood and awkwardly helped Mary clear the table. "I am so sorry, Mary. I was not trying to pry."

Mary's jaw was clenched, all comfort gone. She just wanted Martha to leave, but the woman seemed less inclined to go. Desperately fighting her inner frustration, Mary rushed to the door and gulped in air. Looking off into the distance, she released her heart-cry. "I have to see him again."

Martha came up behind her and touched her elbow lightly. "You mean Jesus?"

Turning to Martha with tears in her eyes, Mary said, "Yes. Martha, I have to see him again." The earnest pleading in her eyes broke the young woman's heart. She knew that feeling so well.

"He's here. Did you know?"

Mary's shocked face showed that she did not. She cried out, "Where?"

"He arrived just this morning. I'm here visiting my aunt, and he and my brother have come to take me back home. My brother, Lazarus, is his best friend."

Searching Martha's face, Mary saw the sincerity, the loving kindness of a friend. She covered her mouth and laughed, shaking with joy at this revelation. Jesus was near, and his friend's sister was standing in her living room.

Mary quickly began moving about the room, grabbing things and throwing them into her bag. She wrapped breads and dried meat and fruits and placed them in a bag, along with sandals and candles, and a blanket. She quickly filled the other bag with clothes, both old and new. All the while she was asking Martha if she could join them, delighting in her affirmative response and flitting about the house grabbing things, flinging some away and putting others in the bag.

Martha watched, amused, as Mary crawled under her bed and retrieved several vases hidden there. She wrinkled her brow at the plain brown clay as the jars were placed on the table, but her jaw fell open when she watched Mary pour one into one bag, and a second into the other. She then emptied a third between the two satchels, slid the fourth toward Martha and kept a fifth near herself.

"You'll help me carry this, right?"

Lazarus's sister gave a slight nod, clearly stunned. Mary hardly noticed. She hoisted a bag onto one shoulder, reached out and grabbed a beautifully adorned box off the mantle and placed it inside on top of her clothing. Before she could grab the other bag, Martha was hefting it onto her own shoulder. Mary grabbed a full vase off the table and gestured for Martha to do the same as she turned toward the door.

Instead of turning up the road to go into town, Mary went instead to her backyard. She set her satchel on the ground and picked up the spade from the spot she dropped it the night before. Kneeling in the soft, overturned dirt, Mary began to dig.

Martha watched as Mary Magdalene dug two holes about a yard apart, fairly deep into the earth. Turning, she picked up a vase and placed it in one of the holes. She stood, looked Martha in the eyes and without explanation, gently took the jar she was holding and placed it in the other hole. Then she knelt and filled the earth in on top of them.

Mary stood, picked up her satchel and, without a word or backward glance, walked around the house to the road. Lazarus's sister watched in wonder, then remembered herself and hurried to catch up with Mary.

The bags they carried were heavy, and Lazarus's sister struggled under the weight of it. But Mary was resolutely determined and seemed to walk taller in spite of the burden. Throwing her hands out as if experiencing freedom for the first time, Mary closed her eyes and inhaled deeply. "I have decided to follow Jesus," she said. "No turning back."

Chapter 11

"How were you carrying this?" Jesus grunted as he shifted the weight of Mary's satchel. Lazarus had taken the bag his sister was carrying, and they were all walking toward the Sea of Galilee.

Mary smiled and shrugged her shoulders.

Lazarus laughed. "No doubt! What do you have in this thing?"

He jostled the bag, and Mary heard a faint jingling. She glanced at Martha and they shared a secret smile, but kept their secret between them.

She was not ready to divulge her plans or her means. In fact, she really had not decided on a definite plan. Martha had simply told the others that Mary was coming to stay as her guest for a while, which explained her bags and her impending time with them.

"I simply cannot allow you to carry this any longer," Jesus teased her.

Mary felt his words in her spirit, which was a new and strange sensation. It was like everything he said to her was full of deeper meanings she hardly understood. She felt his words settle in her soul.

"Come to me, all you who are weary and heavy laden and I will give you rest."

Jesus talked as if reciting his favorite nursery rhyme. Turning to Mary, he said, "Take my yoke upon you, and learn from me. I am humble and gentle at heart, and you will find rest for your souls."

He spoke so directly to her, she felt embarrassed at the intimacy.

With a sly grin, Lazarus interjected, "Hey Jesus, where do you find your rest?"

Jesus laughed as he tossed the satchel over the side of the boat. "In the boat."

Sure enough, shortly after shoving off, and way before everyone was settled, Jesus had thrown himself over their small pile of luggage and fallen asleep. Mary could hear a faint snore, and wondered how he fell so deeply asleep so quickly.

"He's been up for quite a while. Maybe two days straight. I don't know, because I slept, but it seemed like every time I turned around, new people had shown up at the beach to be healed or released." Lazarus leaned in like he had read her mind.

"You were on the beach a few days back, right?"

"Yes," Mary said sheepishly. "I was ... I was there."

Recognition dawned on Lazarus and he smiled widely.

"What is your name?" Like Martha, Lazarus was unabashedly prying, which was uncomfortable, but not altogether unwanted.

"Mary."

"Mary. Right!"

Lazarus delivered a report to her curiosity with much enthusiasm.

"The first night after you left, the beach was full of people who'd come to him to be healed and delivered. Blind men, Mary, received their sight! Men who said they had been blind since birth! And cripples, having never walked or stood, or even eaten on their own, all healed. I saw men walking who had never before even stood up! I saw a woman who'd never walked upright stand straight up, throw away her cane and RUN!"

Lazarus related the last few days' happenings with much animation.

"Those who had no voice began to cry out loudly in praise after being touched by Jesus. After a day on the beach, we went into Chorazin, where a Pharisee had invited Jesus to dine with him. But there were so many people in need, the house was overflowing! It was so full that a group of men tore off the roof to bring their friend to Jesus. They literally tore off the middle of the roof and lowered his entire mat down into the middle of the room, begging Jesus to heal him! Can you imagine that kind of determination and faith?"

His eyes were wild with the memory of the past few days. Mary took it all in as if drawing from a deep well. The two of them were so engrossed in conversation, they hardly noticed the deepness of night descending on them, nor the sudden change in the wind.

The sea became rough and choppy, until finally, the others' concerns drew their attention back to the boat and they realized how reckless the sea had become. A drizzle began to fall and cover everyone and everything in the boat, while the waves lapped over the sides.

Before long, fierce straight-lined winds blew and the passengers clung to the boat and each other. Many of them prayed loudly while huge waves washed over the sides of the boat, coming from every direction. Hard rain drove into their bodies, whipping their clothing and stinging their faces.

Mary clung desperately to Lazarus, his arms wrapped strongly around both herself and Martha. The women huddled together, screaming as the wind threatened to tear them all apart and scatter their pieces on the sea. Many others on the boat braced themselves against the lower planks and screamed out in fear at the violent squall. Amidst their frightened pleas, Mary heard someone scream out, "Jesus!! Master! Don't you care that we perish?!"

The plea cut through Mary's heart; she found it was an echo of her own. Throughout all of it, Jesus remained in the same place, sleeping on a wet pile. Mary turned her head to look at him, expectantly.

Jesus awoke with a start, seeming more disturbed by the disposition of his friends than the storm. He took in the storm and the faces of fear around him, then said without disapproval, "Oh ye of little faith."

Turning to face the raging sea, Jesus raised his hands in the air and rebuked the storm instead. Everything instantly stilled. The wind hushed and the waves ceased. As suddenly as it had started, the storm stopped. At his command.

No one spoke or hardly dared to breathe. Their eyes were all fastened on Jesus. Little murmurs began to ripple through the boat, and for the first time, Mary noticed Judas at the very far end of the bow. Fear dropped from her throat into her gut. He locked eyes with her, licking his lips menacingly. Mary ducked her eyes away and looked back to Jesus. He was perched on the back of the boat, watching the water.

"Who is this man, that even the wind and seas obey him?" A man stared over Mary's shoulder at Jesus. Wonder filled his voice and mirrored her own. Who was this man, indeed?

Chapter 12

The thrust of the boat being forced onto dry land jolted Mary from a disturbed and restless sleep. The men worked together to pull it completely ashore, and the few women left in the boat were in various stages of preparing to disembark.

Mary quickly gathered her things while simultaneously attempting to avoid Judas' penetrating stare. The hatred emanating from his eyes was fearsome and palpable. He did his work with an unflinching glare in her direction.

Panic seized her and Mary looked around, searching for a friendly face. Martha was helping others gather their things, but when she saw Mary, she rushed to her. "Are you okay? You look like you've seen a ghost."

While Mary grappled for an answer to give, Martha positioned the satchels on their shoulders and gathered her brother's things. Mary wondered that she had such a capacity to carry everything. Composing herself, Mary answered, "I'm fine. Where are we?"

"We're in Gadara. We'll set out from here on foot, and walk the rest of the way to Bethany."

"Nonstop?"

Martha laughed, "Relax. No one's in a rush. Jesus likes to visit, so I assume it'll take a few days."

Mary sighed a loud expression of relief. Martha laughed again.

After pulling the boat ashore, the men joined the women who were spread out a short distance away. Together, they shared a small meal before laying down to rest. Mary guessed there were somewhere between 30 and 40 of them, among which she also saw Levi.

She had not seen him the whole time they were in the boat, but having so many on such a relatively small craft, and in the dark, she knew she would not have. She was pleased he was there. An old familiar face filled her with comfort. Even though she knew that at any time, he could expose her, her confidence increased daily because he had not already.

She looked around to see how close Judas was. She noticed him just a short distance away from her, speaking conspiratorially to the man next to him, and looking and gesturing in Mary's direction.

Cutting her eyes away quickly to avoid seeing the man's reaction to whatever was being shared, Mary's heart was instantly full of dread. He was outing her. He was sharing her past and her shame.

Mary's breath quickened to short gasps, and her entire body began to quake in a cold sweat. She shakily stood and stumbled away from the group as heaving sobs overcame her.

Looking up in alarm, Martha glanced frantically between Mary and Lazarus for an indication of what to do. Finally, thoroughly frustrated at her own lack of action, Martha got up to follow her friend. But then Jesus' hand was on her shoulder inviting her to stay as he calmly walked past her to follow Mary.

Jesus found Mary up the hill a ways, huddled against a large boulder and crying out in anguish. His heart was torn by her agony, but aware that he had not been invited, he waited for her to notice him. Her sobs eventually dropped away to a low moaning, then she sniffled. Tilting her head to wipe her face on her sleeve, she noticed Jesus out of the corner of her eye.

"Go away," she said gruffly.

"I ... can't," he said.

Mary looked at him in shock and disbelief. He stood, his eyes fixed on hers and his arms at his sides. Completely comfortable and unflinching.

"What does that even mean?" Mary asked scornfully.

Jesus motioned as if asking to come nearer, but Mary made no indication. Seeing she did not dissuade him, he moved in nearer to her and said, "Your heart ... it's hurting, and I can't just walk away from that."

Mary dropped her eyes to the ground, searching for something to say, but there was nothing.

Finally, "You don't know me."

Pleading, she looked up at Jesus with fresh tears in her eyes and said forcefully, "You don't know what I've done. What I'm like. What I feel on the inside! I'm dying!!"

She sobbed into her hands, covering her face so he could not see the mess she was becoming.

Quietly, gently, Jesus said, "I knew you before I formed you in your mother's womb."

The absurdity of his words were lost on her. Because she felt them in the deepest part of her heart, and she knew what he said was true. As if time were endless, and she and he had been connected forever, and were finally making their way back to each other after years of being lost. Deep peace settled into her heart, but her own fears were there to smother it.

"I'm a whore," she said, without any feeling at all. Looking away, off at the distant sea to avoid his eyes, she continued to spill out her shame.

"I was a child. A child! My daddy told me he loved me. And I knew he did. I was his little girl."

She laughed sardonically. "Until the day he showed me ... in the vilest way."

Her face contorted with the pain of remembering. Tears slid unhindered down her cheeks as she went on. "My momma died, and after that, he sought his comfort from me. He would take me in his bed and hold me while he cried, and then one day-"

Mary's voice dropped off, choked by the shame of what was coming next.

Barely above a whisper, she continued. "When I was falling asleep, safely cuddled next to my father, he kissed me. Then he kissed me again, and it felt different. It felt ... hungry. He started to grope me, and I squirmed away from him. His touch became more persistent and I was afraid. For the first time in my life, I was afraid of my own father. He pressed into me, kissing me, trapping me under his body, and then he touched me in between my legs."

The haunting memory slid behind her eyes, and Mary watched it with a horrified, unmoving stare.

"It felt strange, and good, and awful all at the same time."

She paused, hating the truth but not taking it back inside.

Her voice dropped again. "He kept touching me because I moaned, and he said, 'you like that?' And he took my moaning as permission."

Mary clenched her teeth as she spoke, and then stopped again, her breath arrested by the anxiety of reliving it.

"Then he ... pushed himself inside me."

The look in her eye became wild and frantic, and her words began spilling out like vomit, uncontrollable and fierce.

"I screamed because it hurt, but he didn't stop. He kept moving in me, and I kept screaming, but he never stopped.

He never stopped. It went on forever, until I was numb from the pain, and I had screamed myself hoarse."

She cried, then weakly said, "Finally, he stopped and got up from the bed. But I couldn't move. I wanted to run so bad, but I couldn't even move."

Mary's balled fists pounded out the last few words, mercilessly beating her thighs with each one. Then she released the inner anguish with a piercing scream, her teeth clenched and her body shaking from the rage.

After releasing her anger, Mary looked up at Jesus, afraid of the reaction on his face. She wasn't sure of what she saw there. Was it compassion, or a blank, bored stare? Whatever it was, it looked like he was just waiting for her to finish.

"He even apologized afterward," she said callously.

"But then, he did it again. And again, and again. Then one night, he invited his friend over and after I had gone to sleep, the man came to my bed and ... did it too. I looked past him to my father. I pleaded with him. But he left me. I watched him step out the front door into the night."

She choked in a few deep gulps of air.

"I just gave up." Her voice was flat and unaffected. Jesus could tell that she had indeed given up.

"After that night, it was most nights. Men would come to our house, and my father parceled me out to every last one of them. I slept so little at night, kept awake by either their cravings or my own fearful imaginations. My father took their money and they took me. They took so much of me."

Mary wept bitterly.

"I don't even know who I am anymore! Or who I ever even was!" she spit it out, as if forcing all the anger and hurt out with every word.

"At some point, I put it on as my identity. And after my dad died, I kept them for myself. I took their money and gave them every part of me."

Mary was done. Her story was over, but more than that, she was fully exposed and expecting Jesus to judge the betrayal of her body and the hatred in her heart. She steeled her heart against him, lest his judgment shatter her. She wanted so badly for this man to see the good in her, to find it for her. To call it out like he so effortlessly called out everything else.

Jesus looked at her in deep concentration, as if he were reading the deep things hidden inside.

"Mary, can I tell you a story?"

His voice subdued her emotions, and Mary gave a small nod of assent. Jesus sat down and gestured for her to do the same. Sitting down to face him, Mary instinctively hugged her knees into her body, subconsciously putting a barrier between the two as he began.

"There was a woman clothed with the sun, with the moon under her feet and a crown of twelve stars on her head. She was pregnant, and cried out in pain as she was about to give birth."

Jesus was a methodical story-teller, drawing out the words in just the right places for maximum effect.

"At the time of her travailing, an enormous red dragon appeared, with seven heads and ten horns and seven crowns on its head."

Gesturing with his hands, he displayed the movement of the dragon's tale as he continued, "It was so powerful, its tail swept a third of the stars out of the sky and flung them to the earth."

At this point, Jesus' hands had become just as much a part of the story as his words. He showed her the movement of the dragon and the woman.

"The dragon stood in front of the woman who was about to give birth, so that it might devour her child the moment he was born. She gave birth to a son, a male child, who, it is said, will rule all the nations with an iron scepter."

The tone and pace of his words expressed the climactic change of events as it unfolded. "But before the dragon could destroy the child, he was snatched up to God."

Mary watched Jesus as he spoke. His demeanor had not changed in all the time she had known him, until now. He was as calm and peaceful as he had always been, but he spoke with such authority that she felt like he had personally witnessed this story.

The story was strange, like the many fables her mother told her when she was a little girl. But something about the way he spoke convinced her of its truth.

Jesus took a deep, excited breath and went on. "When the dragon realized it had been defeated, a great war broke out in heaven. Michael and his angels fought against the dragon, and the dragon and his angels fought back. But the dragon was not strong enough. He and his hosts lost their place in heaven. The great dragon was hurled down –that ancient serpent called the devil, or Satan, who leads the world astray. He was hurled to the earth, and his angels with him."

Triumph was in his voice, and the excitement mounted, causing his next words to come trembling out.

"When he saw that he had been hurled to the earth, he pursued the woman who had given birth to the male child, but he was unable to harm her. Instead, because the dragon was enraged at the woman, he went off to wage war against the rest of her offspring."

Mary waited for more, but Jesus was done. He looked at her, waiting, and she did the same to him.

"What does it mean?" she asked him finally.

He held her inquisitive gaze as he explained. "I saw Satan fall like lightening from heaven. He was the seal of perfection, full of wisdom and perfect in beauty. He was in Eden, the garden of God, adorned by every precious stone and anointed as a guardian cherub. He was on the holy mount of God. He was blameless in all his ways, until darkness was found in his heart."

Mary watched as a deep sadness danced with anger behind his eyes.

"He became proud because of his beauty. It was as if he had looked into a mirror and fallen in love with himself. And he said in his heart, 'I will ascend to the heavens; I will raise my throne above the stars of God; I will make myself like the Most High God.' So he was thrown to the earth, and a third of the angels with him. Satan is that dragon, Mary, and he's seeking every day to devour the sons and daughters of God."

Mary was entranced by his story. Captivated. "Who are they?" she asked, innocently.

Jesus smiled at her and said, "How great is the love the Father has lavished on us that *we* should be called sons and daughters of God."

Mary smiled weakly. "And what of the child? Who is he? And why would the dragon want to devour him?"

"The child is the one spoken of in the scriptures."

Jesus looked off into the distance and continued. "The Messiah men have talked about and longed for, for centuries. The one the prophets point to. His destiny is to destroy the work of Satan, to destroy the dragon's power, and the fear that keeps people hidden away in darkness. To destroy the demonic army that rages against mankind, and to bring all the fiery darts of hell down to the dust."

"Where is he?" Mary asked with much longing,

Jesus turned, looked her lovingly in the face and said, "I, the one speaking to you, am he."

Her instant gravitation toward this man suddenly made sense. The joy she found in him, the newness, the peace and security ... Hadn't he already rescued her from darkness? Hadn't he already set her free? Hadn't she found liberty and precious peace in him? Realization dawned on Mary: she was staring into the face of her savior. Jesus.

Chapter 13

A high-pitched screech shattered the stillness between Mary and Jesus. Looking up toward the noise, Mary was surprised to see a man running straight at them, and even more surprised that he was completely naked.

Flailing his arms wildly in every direction, the man came barreling toward them at break-neck speed. Long chains hung off his arms and swung about in the air, striking him on his face and body as he thrashed his arms.

Mary was at once afraid and bewildered. She sprang to her feet behind Jesus, who stood between her and the mad man running at them.

Looking past Jesus, Mary watched the man begin to falter as he ran. The chains seemed to drag him down to the earth as he got nearer and nearer to Jesus, until he staggered and fell, unable to take another step.

Sinking to his knees, the man cried out, "What do you want with us, Jesus, Son of the Most High God?! Have you come to torment us before our time?"

The man pawed at the earth as if in great distress and agony.

"What is your name?" Jesus demanded.

"Legion! For we are many!"

The voice that came out of the man was different this time, deeper and more menacing.

Scooting further back behind Jesus, Mary hugged her arms tightly around herself. The man looked up at Jesus, his facial expressions running through many emotions. Mary could see fear and pain, then anger and fury, then hatred and sadness. The emotions moved across his face so rapidly, and at the same time, words stumbled over his lips.

"Don't hurt me!" the man squealed in terror. But then his terror was replaced with such intense hatred as another, more menacing voice came from the same mouth, screaming insults and curses at Jesus. In the same breath, the man burst into tears, then began groveling in the dirt at Jesus' feet. It was so confusing to watch and as terrified as she was, Mary inwardly grieved for the man behind the masquerade.

Jesus stood patiently, pondering the situation as demons screamed out at him. "Please, Son of God, don't send us into the abyss!"

"Let us go into them!" another frantic voice screeched through the man's mouth as his finger jabbed frantically in the direction of a nearby herd of pigs.

"Go." Jesus spoke in a commanding voice, "Release him immediately!"

Mary heard a loud, metallic pop and watched the chains fall off the man's wrists. A dark fog lifted off him with an unearthly shriek and left the man laying with his face in the dirt, heaving uncontrollably at the feet of Jesus.

Kneeling next to him, Jesus placed a hand on the man's back to calm his convulsions. Taking off his outer robe, Jesus laid it across the man to cover his exposed body. He and Mary turned their heads so the man could wrap himself in it, then they helped him up and all but carried the older man back to the beach.

Mary was surprised to see many of their shipmates standing a short distance away watching the trio with mixed expressions. Some in awe, some in consternation, some in fear.

In a fluid motion, their attentions turned toward a distant outcrop, the sight of a loud clamorous commotion. Dumbstruck, they watched as an entire herd of swine dove one after another off the cliff into the sea. A young boy stood in the field waving his arms frantically and screaming at the top of his lungs. But the pigs did not stop. Every last one of them followed the mad rush ahead into the sea while they all watched helplessly.

Mary and the others were similarly disturbed, although an unperturbed Jesus led them back to their meal at the beach. Excited conversations broke out everywhere and before long, many sat listening to Mary share the man's testimony of deliverance and excitedly explain the suicidal swarm of pigs.

The newest addition to their group clung to Jesus with tears streaming down his face, and begged Jesus to let him come with them. Meanwhile, the food went unnoticed by most.

After a while, the group began to pack up their things. Martha had found an extra garment for the man they had just met, and the two women took him down to the beach and helped him scrub a very thick layer of matted grunge from his body. He was covered in sores and bruises, wounds in various stages of healing, blood and what Mary could only assume was his own waste.

She smiled lovingly at him, though her insides recoiled at the thought of touching him. She kept her eyes on Martha, whose calm, loving demeanor she wished she could replicate. Together they wetted and scrubbed his body until his skin glowed.

The older gentleman sat quietly under their administrations until he was declared clean, then thanked them profusely while they dressed his frail body.

The three of them returned to find a very large, angry group of strangers in the camp. Women were screaming and crying out, their various distresses garbled together and indistinguishable. The men with them were shouting and shaking angry fists at Jesus, who stood stoically, receiving it all yet undisturbed by any of it.

Finally, a man commanded the mob to silence. Pointing an angry finger at Jesus, he demanded to know what had happened to his pigs. His pigs!

The man next to Mary, whom hours before had been under the same cloud of hatred, held out his arms in silent plea as he walked toward them.

"Friends, it's me, James! Don't you recognize me?! I am healed!"

He smiled in triumph, a relatively toothless grin that spread across the lower portion of his face in fervent joy. The crowd gaped at him, momentarily at a loss for words. In fact, no one said a thing. Then a woman in the back cried out, "Has this man once again destroyed my life?"

Flying to the front in a fit of rage, a beautiful, plump middle-aged woman stood angrily with her fists balled up, her arms stick straight at her sides.

"What have you done?" she demanded. Her face was full of fury.

James' arms fell as his eyes searched her uncaring face for some semblance of compassion. His wrists were covered in scars from the fetters he had worn for years, his face freshly wounded by the chains that beat him as he ran down the slopes toward Christ. Here he stood before his own daughter, free and in his right mind, yet still bound by her hatred. His shoulders sagged in defeat and surrender.

Mary, moved by compassion, came to him and put her arm lovingly around his tiny, sickly waist. Passionately, she told the story of his deliverance to an unmoved crowd. Her words fought for understanding from them, but seemed to fall on deaf ears. Deaf ears that only received one bit of it: Jesus was responsible.

The townspeople flew at Jesus, screaming wildly for him to leave immediately. They cursed loudly, creating a curtain of tension between the two groups until finally, Jesus held up his hands. Everyone fell silent.

"I will go."

Again, an uproar ensued, though this time, it slowly moved up the hill in the direction of town. James stood there, listlessly watching them leave. Mary watched too, relieved at their departure.

James tore out from under her arm and threw himself at the feet of Jesus, pleading, "Can I come with you?"

Mary smiled, knowing the ache in his heart. She was startled by Jesus' reply.

"No."

James looked up in disbelief and fear. Mary rushed to Jesus, caught up in echoes of her own despair.

"You must let him!" she cried out. Tears welled up in her eyes. "Jesus, you must. How can you refuse him?"

Jesus' face contorted briefly in pain at her desperation. But then that peace enveloped him, and he knelt gently beside James. "You can't. Because I need you here."

James looked up wearily into the face of Jesus. "No one wants me here."

With such love and tenderness, Jesus said, "But they need you. There are others who need to hear your story. And a daughter's heart that needs restored. And I have given you more than freedom. I have given you a testimony. I give you power and authority to take back what the devil has stolen from you. You must reclaim your land. You must reclaim your family. And you must share your story, because there are many others who need to hear it and believe."

Mary witnessed the transforming power of Jesus' words to James. Strength returned to his body. His shoulders visibly lifted, no longer sagging but strong and wide. His face took shape, his cheekbones returning and his jaw stretching out across his face again. Life and vitality came upon him, and he smiled the smile of a victor. "Ok, I'll go," he said. Then he stood and embraced Jesus.

Chapter 14

The excitement of the day eventually pulled everyone to the earth in exhaustion. Mary picked her way through sleeping bodies to walk the edge of the calm, quiet waters. She was too conflicted to sleep.

Hours before, she had decided to follow Jesus. Left everything behind and pursued him, with reckless abandon. Now, all she could think about was how to get back home.

This was absurd. How did she expect this situation to work out? Eventually, Martha would go back home. She had already told Mary that Bethany was her stop. And then what? Mary had not been invited to stay, and didn't even know that she wanted to.

She knew without a doubt she never wanted to lose sight of this man again. She was just beginning to know him, and through him, to find herself. But she couldn't follow him alone. It was improper, and how could she express the inner desperation for him? She was dying, and he was life. And none of it made sense to her, and she knew it would not make sense to anyone else. So she had to go home.

She had to go home to get away from Judas too. He was tormenting her. His jeers, his hateful glares, and his rampant gossiping, Mary was sure, had spread her reputation all over the camp, even though she was clueless as to how he knew about her past. But he did, and he was telling everyone.

Mary would never overcome their reactions. Their unkind assumptions and the distance they kept bound her to her past, and she felt every moment defeated in a battle she did not even know how to fight. Because it was all true. There was no excuse, and no escape.

She had hoped that things would be different among this group that was following Jesus. She had hoped that they would all be like him, but she quickly found out that they were all more like her … imperfect, to say the least.

"Where are you going?"

Mary turned quickly, and saw his face in the moonlight. That familiar sense of security swept over her, displacing the sudden, gripping fear she felt before she saw him.

"Do you ever sleep?" Mary asked, dismissing his question with a question of her own.

"When I am weak, then He is strong," Jesus said with a wink. Then, he smiled.

"I'm often tired. But the night is long, and there will be time for that later. For now, you need me. And so, here I am."

Mary stopped walking and turned to face him. "How do you do that?"

Jesus didn't respond, but looked back into her eyes boldly.

Mary asked again, "How do you know what I'm thinking, and what I need?" It wasn't an accusation. It was more a marveling question.

Jesus said, "Deep calls unto deep."

Mary knew immediately what that meant, because those few words explained the way her heart reacted to everything he said. But still, she wanted him to explain the phrase.

"Tell me how that works," she said, turning to continue walking along the moonlit beach.

Jesus kept pace with her. "I hear the heart. It is louder to me than all the noise you hear among the crowds. There is a cry from the heart that I always hear. And once I hear it, I hold onto the sound and run after it. Because it means someone is hurting and needs me desperately. I can't let them down. So I run. Every time."

He was so weird. But his words explained so much of her reality that she couldn't quite deny his sanity. Which made her feel insane too.

"That's a little ... bizarre."

Jesus laughed. "Yeah. I know. It doesn't make it any less true, though."

They both got quiet, then Mary felt bold enough to ask him, "Tell me about mine. What did my heart sound like to you?"

Jesus breathed heavily, a look of concern clouding his smile. "When I first ran into you ... literally," he said with a chuckle, "I heard it. It was ... sorrowing. Aching. Crying out."

His face grew serious as he tried to describe the sound of her heart.

"But I heard more than that in you." Looking at her soberly, he said, "I heard them. The torturing, jeering, hateful ambush of Satan's swarm pushing your heart and mind toward the brink. It hurt so bad to see you run away that day."

He said it with such sincerity, Mary felt awkward. Nakedly awkward.

"I was going to kill myself," she said, hoping his reaction was as firm and unmoving as she imagined it would be.

"I know," he said. "That's why I ran after you."

Mary looked at him, trying to discern his meaning. He didn't run after her. But he had never spoken anything besides truth before. "What do you mean?" she asked, almost angrily.

"That day on the hill," he said.

Mary knew what he was talking about. She had run to the brow that morning to kill herself, and a rowdy horde had disrupted her plans.

"The crowd was a pleasant surprise to me too," he said.

"I was pleased that the Father had worked to bring you to me in such a disarming and unassuming way. With or without them, I would have been there that morning. But without them, you may not have received me. All that He does it good," said Jesus, looking in wonder and smiling at the heavens.

Mary followed his eyes heavenward. There were so many questions, she hardly knew which to ask first.

Very meekly, she asked, "You were going to save me?"

Jesus smiled. "Didn't I?"

Mary smiled, then remembering something he had said earlier, she asked, "You heard demons in me?" Her courage faltered under the enormity of the thought. Her shoulders fell and she wrapped her arms around herself to hold herself together.

Looking directly in Mary's eyes, Jesus said tenderly, "There were seven. I saw them, too. Condemnation was coiled around your mind. Pain and Hatred held your heart with bleeding hands. Lust was wrapped around your torso. Perversion was saddled at your hips. And Fear clung to your legs and made you run."

She had never seen anger on his face before. It was both striking and awful. "That was only six," she said, in anticipation.

"Sadness was hidden behind your eyes. And together, they worked on you like master puppeteers."

"How did they get there? And how did I not know?"

"Your past has been a revolving door. Opened in your childhood, it became the entryway for Satan's schemes against you ever since. Demons have had their way in you since the day you were first violated. In you. Through you. Through others."

Mary looked at him, astonished at the revelation, and feeling helpless.

"Why?" she asked weakly.

"For we wrestle not against flesh and blood, but against principalities and powers of darkness and wickedness in high places."

He said it matter-of-factly, which helped Mary to receive it as truth. She knew he was certain of it, and because he was the only thing she was certain about, she believed him.

"Why didn't I know?"

"It is the nature of things to remain hidden." Then he smiled and said, "But it is the nature of light to bring revelation. I am the way, the truth and the light. No one comes to the Father except through me. Do you believe me, Mary?"

Mary said nothing. She thought hard about his words, and let them penetrate her deepest parts.

"I don't know anything truer than you. Something in me agrees with you. Something in me knows you are telling the truth in all things that you say, even though it's all very strange and new. I ... I do."

She said it with such conviction, and then smiled at Jesus. He smiled back, squaring his shoulders in confidence at her words. She turned away from him, unable to hold his gaze another moment without breaking. Then she continued walking as her mind wandered over her latest conundrum: how was she going to get home?

Realizing he was still near her, she turned up the beach toward their party, but then veered off and sat down in the sand, hoping he would keep walking and leave her alone. But she had not understood the nature of Christ: the persistent pursuing in which he followed her and sat down next to her. He remained silent, which unnerved her. The discomfort finally broke her will to hide her intentions and she said, "I'm going home. I can't go on with you."

Jesus looked at her like he already knew. But he still asked, "Why?"

Mary looked at him, resigned, and answered, "I can't."

"Because of Judas?" His frankness surprised her, but not as much of his awareness of the situation that was robbing her of peace.

"How did you know?"

Disregarding her question, Jesus said, "There are those who are pure in their own eyes, and yet are not cleansed of their filth. Take heart, for whoever conceals their sin does not prosper, but the one who confesses and renounces them finds mercy. You, Mary, have found mercy. That will not be taken from you."

Mary longed to feel free from the condemnation of Judas and the others. She didn't want to carry the weight of her past any longer. But their gossip and their rejection was a burden she could not carry. It pulled her down into a pit she had just been pulled out of, and she had to escape.

"I know," she said, "I know what I have found in you. But they won't let me keep it if I stay. I cannot bear to lose this freedom."

She started to cry, hoping he could hear her heart speaking words she could not quite get out: How badly she needed to stay. How scared she was, both to stay and to leave. The fear of reliving her past through their condemning stares and hateful words.

Jesus stood, and she thought he was going to leave her at last. But she was no longer wishing him away. She was desperate for him to stay. To avoid seeing him walk away, she buried her face in her hands and wept, pouring out the devastation in her heart. To her surprise, he touched her shoulder then held out his hand.

"Shake off your dust. Rise up. Sit enthroned! Free yourself from the chains on your neck, daughter, now captive."

Mary was so comforted by his words. Like a prisoner lifted out of a deep pit, his firm hand helped her stand up so that she was facing him. Their eyes locked and their bodies mirrored each other. Her hand rested in his and with his other hand, Jesus gently wiped her tears away.

"Do not be afraid, you will not be put to shame. Do not fear disgrace, you will not be humiliated. You will forget the shame of your youth. Instead of your shame, you will receive a double portion, and instead of disgrace, you will rejoice in your inheritance. And everlasting joy will be yours."

Mary drank in his words like cold, quenching water. They filled her, satisfying the thirsty soul inside and wetting the driest places in her arid heart, reviving her. She closed her eyes to focus on the way his words drowned out the ache of a life-long drought.

"I will contend with those who contend with you."

Courage swelled up in Mary. She felt the safety of his words, the comfort of a friend and a protector. She felt strong in him. Appreciated his strength in the place of her weakness. She felt sure of him and knew she would go on in spite of her fears and intimidation, or the reactions of the others. This man was a rock, and she had decided to trust his steadfastness, to cling to him.

Chapter 15

After a second, lazy day on the beach and another restful night, the group packed up and headed south toward Nain. The anatomy of the group had changed as some had set off in the boat, and others climbed the mountainous hill to Gadara. In exchange, villagers from Gadara had joined their gang of sojourners for the long trek to Jerusalem.

Mary and Martha had reached a rhythm in their friendship, and began sharing more freely with one another. Martha was surprised to know the deeper thoughts and feelings of her new friend, but delighted that Mary trusted her enough to be so open. In return, Mary learned new things about Martha. For instance, that Martha and Lazarus were the oldest of a trio of siblings. Their younger sister, Mary, had been left in the care of a close relative in Bethany. Although she was a young adult, she was very carefree and naïve and her older siblings thought it would be best to have her stay close to home while they were away. In the company of many strangers, and most being men, they had feared for her safety. Of course, convincing her to stay had not been easy. Especially when she found out Jesus would be accompanying them.

"Mary is very fond of Jesus," Martha told her. "She will sit for hours listening in fascination to his teachings. Almost to the point of impropriety," Martha said, rolling her eyes. "Not that Jesus notices. But I do. Am I not also a woman?" she said with a small laugh.

The two talked comfortably as the group walked. There was a lifetime of untold things between them that they enjoyed uncovering for each other. It felt nice to Mary to find another human being who shared similar joys and fears, faults and all.

The group moved like a churning amoeba, and at one point Mary got a whiff of a man walking heavily in front of them which caused her stomach to turn. Self-consciously, she lifted up her arm as discreetly as possible and took a short sniff. The smell was a powerful reminder that she was overdue for a bath. She half coughed, half laughed and said quietly to Martha, "Martha, I think we stink."

Martha lifted up her own arm, and her face showed how pungent the odor was. She wrinkled her nose and nodded her head. Then she nudged the woman next to her and whispered under her breath. Soon, all the women had assessed themselves and a tiny uproar among them ensued. Shortly after, the group passed a small stream, and the majority insisted they stop there before entering Nain, just ahead of them.

The men settled down around a fire a short, discreet distance away. Seeking out the shelter of trees to hide from prying eyes, the women began to undress and dip into the stream. From one direction came a coveted bar of soap, from another came a cheap bottle of perfume. The women splashed and giddily washed themselves, rubbing the soap and oil into their hair and skin. The fragrance settled upon the water and created an alluring atmosphere that drew them out of their collective shell and into a romping, playful mood.

Mary snuck away to her things and grabbed the expensive bottle she had tucked away into her bag before leaving home. She took it back to the water and motioned for Martha to come closer. She was unwilling to share it with all the women, but wanted to invite her friend to enjoy the prize. This perfume had been passed down from her mother, and Mary had never even used it. She remembered her mother wearing it on special nights, right before handing Mary off to her neighbor and slipping out the door with her husband.

Mary closed her eyes and remembered the scent of it on her mother's neck. She smiled with longing, then uncapped the bottle and put a small dab of it behind her ears and on her wrists. She invited Martha to do the same before sneaking back to the beach to re-tuck it in the bag.

Taking their garments to the edge of the river, Mary and Martha washed them, allowing the water to run off their wrists and carry the sweet smell of calamus and cinnamon to their clothing. After every trace of mud and dirt had been washed out, Mary and Martha hung their clothing over a low-hanging branch and sat on the beach exposed and happily clean, comfortable with each other and unafraid of their shared vulnerability. They gnawed a piece of fruit Mary had been hanging on to, and laughed and talked while their garments dried in the midday sun.

The rest of the group left them alone to themselves for the most part. Most of the women seemed less comfortable with the open air touching their naked bodies, and so instead of washing their clothing, many had shimmied back into their dirty clothes and hurried back to the camp. A few had stayed, but kept discreetly away from the others. It surprised Mary when an older woman approached the two and sat down. She kept her eyes averted from them for a long time, and when she finally did look up, it was directly into Mary's eyes as she said, "Why are you here?"

Her frankness surprised Mary, as did the way she said it. It was an innocent question, seemingly full of concern, and forced out as if she was aware that it was uncouth. Martha and Mary looked at her in shock. Mary began to stutter out a reply she hadn't quite figured out in her mind when Martha rushed to her aid:

"Mary, this is Salome. She is the mother of James and John, whom if you haven't met yet, are friends of Jesus." Turning a reprimanding eye to the other woman, she said gently, "Salome, this is Mary. My friend. Also a friend of Jesus."

Salome received Martha's reprimand without acknowledging it. "You'll have to forgive my frankness. It is customary where I come from to not hide behind niceties when a concern needs to be addressed. And I am concerned."

Mary looked down at her hands as if they were engaged in the most fascinating foreplay to avoid Salome's hard stare. She tried hard to come up with something to an answer, but it was easy to see she was failing. Again, Martha came to her rescue.

"Why are you concerned, Mother?" she asked, giving Salome the usual greeting of a younger women to the elder. Fully acknowledging the seat of wisdom Salome held, and silently praying she held it with honor.

Salome's eyes stared hard into Mary as Mary lifted her head to take on the threat in front of her. She had decided to follow Jesus, and she knew the price it might cost was higher than anything she had ever gone through before. So she decided to pay it with her head held high.

Mary met her eyes and fought the urge to run from her stare again. Salome went on. "Do you know, Martha, who she is? Do you even know why she is here? As a mother, I find it a brazen way for a woman in her position to work up clientele."

Struggling to maintain her composer, Martha's confidence faltered at the implication Salome was suggesting. "What do you know of her?"

Mary kept her eyes on Salome. Her heart was beating fast, and she was struggling to maintain her grip on her composure. She kept silent.

Salome's voice came out in a whisper, "She's a prostitute, Martha. A prostitute! And she's following a holy man, who is surrounded by a bunch of other men. Imagine the notches on her bedpost after this conquest! Imagine her purse after hanging around this group of vulnerable men for a while. Imagine the victory of seducing Jesus!"

She said this last part with such bitter distaste. Then she implored, "I am a mother, Martha! My sons are here. I have a right to be concerned!"

Salome defended herself vehemently, her eyes darting between the solid stare of Mary and the concerned and seemingly disgusted face of Martha.

The three women remained silent for a few seconds until Mary spoke. Grabbing Martha's hand, she kissed it and said, "It's true, Martha. You can believe her, because she has no reason to lie to you. I, on the other hand, have wished to keep my past from you because I wanted more than anything to enjoy your company and friendship. I have never had a friend before."

Her voice cracked with emotion, and tears began to roll down her face. "I was a prostitute. Before. Before I met you, and before I came here. I have wanted more than anything to escape my past and find refuge among the people who follows Jesus. I thought I had, actually."

She cut her eyes toward Salome and looked at her with hurt evident on her face. Salome seemed unforgiving, afraid to let this woman's cries penetrate her fortress.

Looking back to Martha's concerned face, she continued, "But I could not. It is ever before me, and chasing me. And although I don't want it anymore, I am continually overtaken by my own shameful reputation."

It was Martha's decision to make on how to respond to her friend's anguished cries. Mary sighed heavily and wept into her hands. Salome looked away, a wave of hot guilt washing over her cold heart. Martha reached out and tremulously touched Mary's quivering back.

"I'm so sorry. I'm sorry you carry this with you."

Although Mary appreciated Martha's response, she finally felt the strength in her legs to carry her away from the situation. She stood, hastily dressed and walked away, hearing the beginnings of what she hoped was a tongue lashing on her behalf. The anger she felt inside her was not new, it was just uncovered and revived.

Storming toward the fire, Mary sat down heavily beside Jesus, who was sitting off by himself. She felt like a child, and knew at once her intrusion. But her heart yearned for the safety and comfort she found in being near him, and she had acted without forethought. He looked up at her, searching for a clue as to what was wrong, but only smiled and said nothing.

Mary reacted instantly, "I'm not trying to seduce you."

Jesus laughed lightly. "You don't have to try to seduce anyone."

"What does that mean?!" Mary asked, horrified.

Jesus looked off at the horizon. "You are a beautiful woman. And so seduction is not something you necessarily have to work at."

He picked up a stick and started jabbing the dirt in front of him. Mary was mortified. She had not come to entice anyone, and found comfort in the fact that no one saw her that way ... except for maybe Judas.

"I didn't want to seduce you either."

"I know," Jesus said nonchalantly

Mary became insistent, "Well, did I?"

"There are three things that are too amazing to me," said Jesus, looking at her. "Four that I do not understand. The way of an eagle in the sky, the way of a snake on a rock, the way of a ship on the high seas, and the way of a man with a young woman."

Mary blushed, unsure of his meaning and embarrassed by his gaze. "Who does?" she said, to allay the awkward feeling wedged between them.

Jesus laughed again and said, "It is natural, I think, for a man to react to a beautiful woman. Women are created to entice men. All of God's creatures are created to coexist in such a way. One alluring and seducing the other. It's how species propagate. Your seductive nature is innate." He smiled at her, which somewhat put her at ease.

"But I didn't intend to do that to you. Or anyone here," she said frantically.

"I know," Jesus said. He kept poking the stick into the dirt, and Mary watched him just to have something to look at besides his face.

"Well did I?!" she insisted.

Jesus looked at her again and answered, "If you are asking me if I noticed your beauty, then yes. If you are asking if I had a natural physical reaction to your femininity, the answer is yes. Those things are not a sin. And it's not necessarily something you have control of. The sin, Mary, would be either of us reacting to our physical urges, or you or I intentionally chasing down the pleasure of those urges. I do not look at you to be enticed. And you do not chase after me to be lusted after. And your being here is not for pleasure such as some suggest."

"So you know what they are saying about me?" she asked, defensively.

"Yes." He said it as if he were apologizing, which disarmed her a little.

"What do I do?" she cried out.

"In quietness and trust will be your strength," Jesus replied calmly.

Mary pondered his words before asking, "So I should ignore them?" The thought made her angry. "I should just act like everything they are saying about me, all the assumptions and the gossiping are okay? Are they okay with you?!" she demanded.

Jesus looked at her, unaffected by her anger. "No, it's not okay with me. But I did not come to judge the world. My ways are higher ways."

Mary thought about that and then said, "You said you would contend with those who contend with me." She clenched her teeth and spoke through them, "They are talking about me, slandering me. I am trying to escape my past and they are dragging it behind me forcing me to look at it and live under it again!"

Jesus looked at her with compassion evident and said, "Do not look to the right or the left. Look at me. I accept you. I have called you. Drawn you with cords of loving kindness. I am the reason you are here. Not them. Keep your eyes steadfastly on me."

Mary asked wearily, "How do I overcome it?"

Jesus stood and looked at her. "By the blood of the lamb and the word of your testimony."

Mary was confused. She furrowed her brow. "The blood of the lamb? Wha- what is my testimony?"

"What indeed," Jesus mused, and walked toward the fire, leaving Mary to contemplate his words.

Chapter 16

Mary walked the rest of the way to Nain by herself. She carefully avoided the ever-increasing number of people who knew of her past, although she ached for Martha's friendly smile and easy conversation.

She knew where each of them were. Salome walked several paces ahead of her, nearer to Jesus, trying to pull him into conversation as they walked. Jesus seemed otherwise lost in thought, though he did not dismiss her attempts to talk to him. Judas was also in front of her, walking near the opposite side of the group from Mary. She walked behind him so that he could not look at her without being obvious about it. Martha was somewhere behind her, and Mary made sure the distance remained between them by walking faster when she caught the sound of Martha's voice on the wind. Avoiding them all was a delicate balancing act. She had forgotten, however, that Levi was also among them.

"I noticed you were all alone. Are you okay?"

Mary looked at him and stepped away to put more distance between them.

"I'm okay," she said, looking ahead to avoid signaling any interest in the conversation.

Levi kept stride with her, even as her pace quickened.

"Oh ... okay," he said awkwardly. "Sorry if I'm intruding. I just thought since we're both here, and you don't know many people ..."

He looked at the side of her face, wondering at her disengaged body language. "I don't know what I was thinking." He got quiet and slowed down a little, letting her outpace him so they could part ways without seeming obvious.

As they neared Nain, a loud commotion interrupted the conversations around her. Jesus led the way into the city, and their large band of travelers ran straight into a funeral procession headed out of town. Wailing women surrounded the pallet being carried on the shoulders of four men, a motionless young boy on top of it.

A woman near the front of the procession was not merely paying lip service to the deceased. She was doubled over in grief, moaning loudly in her distress. The others, less sincere, raised their voices to match her fervent pitch and altogether drowned her out.

Mary watched her, recognizing her pain, and so caught the sight of Jesus approaching her through the crowd. She thought of the woman's heart-cry and wondered what it sounded like to him.

Jesus reached out to the anguished woman and touched her shoulder. She lifted her face to him, as if his touch had shocked her. Her eyes met his and her voice got quiet. The wailing around them dissipated until it was relatively silent, and everyone near her heard Jesus say, "What is it, Mother?"

"My son," she said, overcome again with grief.

"Your only son?"

"My only son," she confirmed through broken sobs.

"Don't cry," Jesus said gently, and then turned to the bearers. Mary could see that he was holding back tears as he motioned to the men to stop. No one moved. They were all transfixed on Jesus, waiting and watching in expectation.

Jesus touched the bier that the body was on and said, "Young man, I say to you, get up."

All eyes turned to the bier. A cough tumbled from the lips of the dead boy, who rolled over to his side and weakly pushed himself up to a sitting position. A loud, collective gasp emitted from the mass of onlookers, startling the boy, who frantically insisted for his mother.

His mother stood frozen in awe by the miracle. Someone reached out to nudge her forward, which broke the spell and she fell to her knees weeping with such relief and joy.

Jesus lifted the boy off the pallet and placed him in her eagerly outstretched arms. Pulling her son in, the mother began showering him with kisses and hugs. Tears of joy poured from her as she embraced her son, and he his mother.

The mourners watched in wonder, speaking in hushed excitement. Dropping the bier, the pallbearers ran in every direction shouting emphatically about the miraculous healing. Because of their witness, the number of onlookers grew quickly. Before long, it seemed that the entire town had come to the site.

Mary felt an inner ache as she watched and listened to the boy's story traveling the length and width of the jubilant crowd. She smiled weakly at the excited people around her while her eyes fought the crowd to find Jesus. The panic in her heart reminded her that she had to keep her eyes on him regardless of the joyful raucous around her.

This man had become her security. Her safe place. She felt rooted and strong when she was with him. The fact that there was nothing sexual between them gave her confidence that he was there solely because he wanted to be, which was foreign to Mary. She didn't have to earn his attention or affection. She didn't have to woo him. She wasn't even chasing him because Jesus wasn't running. He was being and she was being and from that came a natural friendship that she needed so much.

Jesus did not escape the people. They pushed toward him from every direction with all kinds of needs and ailments. He smiled lovingly and touched each one, saying, "According to your faith, let it be done unto you."

Mary watched as men and women blinked their eyes for the first time and excitedly pointed out faces and people they had only ever known by the sound of their voices. Laughter rose above the crowd, mingled with praises to God.

A pile of canes grew beside Jesus as others limped to him, received his touch and ran away shouting praises at the top of their lungs. The joyful noise was awful and exciting all at once. Mary took it in in astonishment.

A few days later, their journey finally ended at Bethany. Mary accompanied Martha and Lazarus to their home, and was delighted that Jesus was also resting there.

Waves of relief swept through her, driving out the fear and anxiety she had suffered under in the uncertainty of where Jesus might be going. For the first time in many nights, Mary was able to sleep deeply and peacefully, her heart comforted by the nearness of her savior.

Chapter 17

The next morning, Mary awoke to loud, obnoxious banging noises coming from the kitchen. She had fallen asleep next to Martha, but Martha was no longer beside her. Throwing her clothes on, she hurriedly rushed into the kitchen.

To her surprise, it was only Martha, but she looked angry and she was making quite a fuss out of cleaning up the kitchen. Mary wondered how to approach her friend. She had never seen her in such a mood before.

Before she could say anything, Martha looked up at her and breathed heavily. She shot Mary a fake, tight smile and stormed over to the doorway to peer into the other room. Mary's eyes followed her and took in the intimate sight of Jesus talking to a younger woman.

The woman's eyes were transfixed on Jesus, and he gazed at her lovingly while he spoke to her. Mary ached, recognizing the intimacy between them and certain that if felt like they were the only two people in the world.

The woman smiled sweetly as he talked. She was sitting on the floor at his feet, and he was bent down, sharing a story with her. His eyes were bright and wide, his face animated by the tale. Mary found it hard to pull her eyes away from the scene before her, but then Martha walked into the room and stood with her arms crossed next to the younger woman. All eyes were on her as she said in a strained voice, "Lord, don't you care that my sister has left me to do all this work by myself? Tell her to help me!"

Mary was surprised by Martha's effrontery. The younger Mary and Jesus both turned their heads toward Martha. Jesus' face was full of tender love and care.

"Martha, you are worried and upset about many things, but few things are needed. Actually, only one. Mary has chosen what is better, and it will not be taken away from her." He smiled down at Mary.

Martha turned and stormed back into the kitchen, grumbling to herself. Mary Magdalene stood in the doorway with mixed feelings. She felt the pain and anxiety of Martha, but longed for the rest and joy her younger sister was experiencing at the feet of Jesus.

Feeling awkwardly caught in the middle, Mary decided to go outside. Slipping out the door without notice, she wandered down the path in front of the house. A small family garden graced the far edge of the yard and Lazarus was there pulling up weeds and foraging for the few small vegetables that survived their recent absence.

He wiped the sweat off his brow with a dirty hand and then coughed roughly, his chin forcefully thrust down into his chest. Mary watched him strain with the force of hacking, and was alarmed until he abruptly stopped and returned to his work.

"What's everyone preparing for?" she asked loud enough for him to hear.

Lazarus looked up at her and smiled. "This evening, we've been invited to dine with Simon, a local Pharisee. My sister Martha is somewhat famous for her hospitalities, so even though we go to his house to dine, she will serve the guests."

With a laugh he said, "I guess you heard her in the kitchen looking for something to cook with. I'm looking for something to cook."

"And that must be your younger sister, Mary, in there with Jesus."

Lazarus smiled, "Yes, that's Mary. Ever at the feet of Jesus. She adores him."

"As anyone can tell," Mary said, without envy. She glanced in the window and saw Jesus and Mary laughing together. She smiled with longing.

Lazarus stood and brushed himself off, then picked up the basket of vegetables. Suddenly, his body was seized with hacking again, and he stumbled forward. Mary rushed in to catch his weight and keep him from falling or dropping the basket.

"Thank you," he said after composing himself. Mary smiled in reply.

"Now I'm off to rescue my sister," Lazarus said with a twinkle in his eye.

Mary watched him go and a warm smile spread through her. She liked the sense of normalcy she felt with these people. No one treated her like an outcast, no one accused her, and no one desired her. It was refreshing.

****

That evening, Mary found herself alone at Martha's house. She'd been invited to dinner, but so had the rest of the town and Mary was not feeling up to the company. She just wanted to be alone with her thoughts.

She had met Mary, Martha's sister, and was immediately delighted by her youth and innocence. She had spent the day in the kitchen, trying to connect with Martha, but thoroughly distracted by Jesus's voice in the other room. She strained to hear him over the din of preparation and Martha's excited chatter about the upcoming dinner party. She smiled absently, and was relieved that Martha was too full of conversation to notice. Now that everyone was gone, Mary was able to breathe and think.

Something about the miraculous healing in Nain nagged at her. Something about the reaction of those who witnessed it unsettled Mary. It was their joy. The way they celebrated when the young lifeless body lived again ... she wanted that.

She had felt dead inside, hadn't she? And now, she felt alive! She felt revived, as if she had been brought back to life. And Jesus did that for her just like he did it for the child. But the awe of the people was short-lived.

Those who had witnessed it were gone, and no one else knew her joy. Martha had not seen her spectacular deliverance, and they did not celebrate the freedom found in Jesus anymore. They had settled into a familiarity that was almost mundane compared to the inexpressible joy Mary had when she first met him. She missed the joy, and once the memory of it was awakened, she ached for it. And she immediately wanted to pursue it again, take hold of it and wrap it around herself.

She thought about Mary, the younger woman who sat all day at Jesus' feet and gazed up at him with fervent adoration. About her innocence. Mary longed for that too. She so desired the acceptance and freedom she knew Mary must feel from Jesus, to sit idly at his feet all day while the household went on without her.

Mary sighed heavily, wishing to love herself with such confidence. Her own name, Mary Magdalene, was spoken in a whisper as if it were a curse men should not speak. And yet, here was another Mary who lived with such reckless abandon, it was intoxicating just to watch her. She smiled, she laughed, she lived.

Mary buried her head in her arms and wept for freedom again. It had come this far in mitigating gasps, and Mary finally just wanted freedom to come as easily as breath itself. She wanted to know freedom like Mary knew it. She wanted to be that Mary. A new Mary. A new anybody except Mary Magdalene.

Chapter 18

Mary followed the silence in the streets until it ran into rambunctious cacophony near the outskirts of the city. She knew instinctively this was where they were. The whole town at large. That was the kind of crowd that always surrounded Jesus. He had to pull himself away from people, because humanity itself was drawn to him. And even though the faces and the needs that surrounded him changed, he was always surrounded when in public. Mary knew she had found the house of Simon the Pharisee.

She moved slowly, unnoticed, through the people pressing into the open doorway. She was small and, with little effort, managed not to make waves as she skirted the outer wall and slid into the house. All eyes were straining to catch a glimpse of Jesus, therefore no one noticed the beautiful, olive-skinned woman with piercing golden eyes slip past one after another to scoot closer to the right side of the table, where Jesus sat at the right hand of Simon.

Standing with her back pressed against the wall, she hardly dared to breathe. She wondered how they all did not hear her heart pounding in her chest. She had no excuse for being there, and definitely no invitation. Her heart compelled her near him.

There was so much noise, so much conversation, so many things going on to draw their attention away from her. A servant rushed past her toward the kitchen, in a hurry to get more wine on the table. This meeting could last well into the night, and his master could not afford to stain his reputation as a host by dishonoring such a guest.

Mary closed her eyes and silently prayed that the servant did not recognize her. Thankfully, his eyes were full of apprehension, and could not grasp the memory of her.

Exhaling silently, she inched her way closer to the table, trying harder and harder to not bring attention to herself. How in the world had she ever come this far, she wondered.

She looked around the room at the others. Men surrounded the table, lounging over chairs, on rugs, in the dirt. Every one riveted to the conversation at hand. Women, not commonly invited to dine with the men, were engaged in whispery conversations scattered along the edge of the room. So many distractions, so much to be thankful for.

Mary moved silently, unnoticed, toward Jesus. Her head was down and her fingers wrapped tightly around the gift she had brought for him. Determination moved her along the wall toward him, inch by inch.

The moment she came up directly behind him, bodies began shifting like the parting of the Red Sea her mother used to tell her about, and somehow, there was room for her to move nearer still. She said a silent prayer for courage and rushed to Jesus' feet.

Shame swooped in to attack her, but fell back into Fear at Jesus' penetrating gaze. He had noticed her. There was no way Shame and Fear could work against her now. But Disdain and Accusation were still standing sentinel near the homeowner. Satan had not altogether lost his moment.

The noise in the room tapered off into a terrifying silence as Mary Magdalene fell at Jesus' feet, tears falling shamelessly. Years of anguish and torment found relief in that moment.

She kissed his feet. How could she express her love for him? She wept freely, removing the shroud that covered her head and letting her hair fall down her back.

The room let out one low, collective gasp. She hardly noticed. Jesus sat watching her as she cried, watching her as she began wiping the tears off of his dusty feet with her beautiful, clean hair. His human heart could hardly contain the joy and adoration. If only she knew how much he loved her.

The room erupted as she pulled out an expensive bottle of perfume. Whispers of excitement, of condemnation and resentment filled the air with noise and created a circle of intimacy around Jesus and Mary. Only he could hear her groaning heart pour itself out at his feet.

Judas, driven to his feet in rage, furrowed his brow in consternation. How had she gotten in? Who let her through the door? How had no one noticed her before she got to Jesus? He pressed his jaw together firmly. The smell of perfume did nothing to assuage him. His hardened heart could not accept the glorious reality of what was happening at the other end of the table.

Bowing her head down, Mary kissed Jesus' precious feet, then opened the bottle and poured out the perfume. The last thing of value she owned. Completely oblivious to the audience in the room, she lovingly rubbed the perfume into the calluses on his feet. She kissed his feet again, and again wiped them with her hair.

Tears of joy and deliverance poured from her, down her face, dripping onto his feet and then down onto the floor as Mary emptied herself of years of pain and shame. Jesus gazed down at her in love.

Simon couldn't contain his indignation any longer. Judas had told him about this woman, and the recognition was immediate. A harlot, in his house! He stood abruptly and slammed his hand down on the table. This is exactly the thing Jesus would bring into his home! Hadn't he known that?

"Jesus! She's a whore! How could you let her touch you?!"

Jesus bent down, gently touched her chin to lift her face toward his. "I forgive you."

Mary's heart swelled and leapt. Her eyes reverberated a gleam they had not known since her youth. Joy filled her. Forgiveness crowned her while tears ran down her radiant face.

Jesus looked up and around the table. Mary lowered her eyes back to the floor, still embracing the hardened feet of the man who continually caressed her heart with his love.

"Simon, I have something to tell you," Jesus said.

"Tell me, teacher," Simon answered sarcastically.

All eyes moved from Mary to Jesus. "Two people owed money to a certain moneylender. One owed him five hundred denarii, and the other fifty. Neither of them had the money to pay him back, so he forgave the debts of both. Now, which of them will love him more?"

"I suppose the one who had the bigger debt forgiven," answered Simon.

"You have judged correctly," Jesus said. The he turned toward Mary and continued, "Do you see this woman? I came into your house. You did not give me any water for my feet, but she has wet my feet with her tears and wiped them with her hair. You did not give me a kiss, but this woman has kissed my feet many times. You did not put oil on my head, but she has poured perfume on my feet. Therefore, I tell you, her many sins have been forgiven, as her great love has shown. But whoever has been forgiven little loves little."

Jesus looked Mary in the eyes. A look that lifted her spirits from the pit of despair. "Your sins are forgiven. Your faith has saved you. Go in peace."

Mary stood and turned, about to walk back out of the room when Judas announced with much hostility, "That perfume could have been sold, and the money given to the poor!"

Before Mary could even consider a response, Jesus said, "Leave her alone! Why are you bothering her? She has done a beautiful thing to me. The poor you will always have with you, and you can help them anytime you want. But you will not always have me. She did what she could. She poured perfume on my body beforehand to prepare me for burial. Truly I tell you, wherever the gospel is preached throughout the world, what she has done will also be told, in memory of her."

Mary's heart soared. Jesus had publicly exonerated her. She glanced up into his face and felt his smile impressed upon her soul. Turning again toward the door, she walked out through a parted crowd, no longer afraid or concerned about their opinions. Jesus had once again set her free.

Chapter 19

"Mary, are you coming along with us?"

Jesus stood at the door of Martha's house looking in at Mary's anxious face. She knew her silence had betrayed her. All the others stood wishing him luck at his parting, and Mary stood behind the rest wringing her hands and saying nothing.

Tears welled up in her eyes at the thought of Jesus leaving. She wanted to go so badly, but Martha and Lazarus were staying behind with their sister, and Mary had not been invited by either group.

Her eyes widened at his question and she began to mutter out an excuse, but Martha came up behind her and grasping her elbow. "Yes, of course Mary! You should go! Jesus is going back toward Capernaum, and I am sure he would be willing to take you back home."

Mary knew Martha meant well by her suggestion but "home" was the last place Mary wanted to go. She wanted desperately to stay with Jesus, no matter where it took her. But she also knew the impropriety of it, and did not want to seem too eager.

"Mary?" Jesus said again, startling Mary out of her racing, wondering thoughts.

"I – I'd love to go," she said shyly.

Her things had never been unpacked, and were already by the door, so she moved toward them but again Jesus picked them up and said teasingly, "I could never let you carry these."

Jesus smiled and hugged the neck of his best friend and his sisters. The younger Mary threw her arms around his neck and nearly tipped him over with the force of her hug. She cried freely into his neck, then kissed his cheek and turned to hug Mary.

Throwing a heavy arm around Mary's neck, Martha said with tears, "I hate to see you go. Please, please come back soon. It's been so refreshing, having you here." She released Mary and wiped tears from her cheeks, smiling with longing at the thought of losing her new friend.

Mary and Jesus turned and walked out of the house with fresh tears in their own eyes. They joined a small group of men and women at the end of the dirt path leading up to Lazarus' house, and the group headed northwest toward Jerusalem.

"Mary, may I ask you something?" Jesus began, after they had walked several minutes in silence at the back of the small band of travelers.

"Sure ... I guess so," Mary said, with less certainty than she tried to convey.

"Why do you constantly feel like you have to pay penance to feel accepted by me and free from your past?"

His question was so straightforward, it hit Mary in the gut like a well-aimed fist.

"What do you mean?" she asked anyway, hoping for time to analyze herself for an answer.

"I, the Lord, search the heart and mind," he quoted with a gentle smile. "You have come to me many times hoping to be set free, when in fact I set you free in the beginning. Do you remember me saying to you, 'whom the son sets free is free indeed'? But you do not feel free, and that keeps you running back to me with a new way to earn it."

Without her will or her consent, Mary was open and bare before him. He understood her inner thoughts and reasoning, which was both vulnerable and liberating. Aware that she couldn't fool him even if she wanted to, she simply shrugged and said, "Guilty as charged."

"You do know you are free, don't you? That I accept you and have set you free from your past. You don't have to carry it around anymore."

For emphasis, Jesus jiggled her bag strap, and Mary heard a soft jingling sound that was literally the wages of her sin. Hoping to alleviate the growing anxiety in her, she jokingly said, "I don't. You do."

A loud, awkward laugh erupted from her and then her face turned red and she quickly lowered it to avoid his amused reaction.

"Did you just make a joke?" he asked with a laugh.

Mary looked up to search his face for any negativity, but he was looking at her with delight. She laughed back, feeling more alive from the ease developing between them.

"So this is it, then? Your constant reminder?" Jesus said, indicating the bags he held.

Mary felt boldness well up in her. She trusted him to accept what she said without accusation or condemnation, so she said, "Yes, that. And him," she said, pointing ahead of them at Levi. "And him," she said more severely as she pointed next to Judas. "And this," she said, indicating her purple shawl and her clothing. "And my name," she said, a tremor escaping through her lips as she said it.

"Your name?" He asked innocently.

"Yes, my name. I'm Mary Magdalene. Try it out in a synagogue and see what kind of reaction you get," she said sarcastically. "I'm known all over Israel. Men traveled from far and near for my embrace. Women cringe at the thought of me. I hate my name."

Locking eyes with Jesus, she dropped her defenses and let him read her soul. She had no more secrets and would not have kept them anyway. There was such liberation in the candidness of their conversation.

"My mother's name is Mary," Jesus said like he missed every revealing thing Mary had just admitted. "I think Mary's a good name." He smiled and Mary smiled back.

"Maybe for a good woman," she replied. "For instance, Lazarus' sister. She's so innocent and loving. So pure. And your mother. I'm sure she was pure and devoted to her husband."

"My mother is a saint," Jesus said smiling. "But not many people know that. My mother is accused of having a child out of wedlock. She was pregnant with me before she married my dad."

Mary gasped at the revelation. Jesus remained unmoved by her reaction. "She was guilty in the eyes of the world too." He smiled and breathed deeply before he said, "But they are wrong about her just like they are wrong about you."

"How were they wrong about her?" Mary asked. "Wasn't she guilty?"

"Therefore the Lord himself will give you a sign: the virgin will conceive and give birth to a son."

Mary gaped. "More of the prophecies?" she asked incredulously.

Jesus smiled again, winking at her. Mary couldn't take her eyes off him. The revelation coursed through her like new wine. Finally she said, "Ok, but I am not innocent. In their eyes or in reality. I am guilty"

Jesus stopped walking and caught her arm to stop her. His eyes bore into her, still flooding her with compassion as he asked, "Who shall lay anything to the charge of God's elect?"

"But it's true!" she insisted, her lips quivering with a fresh wave of guilt.

"Behold, old things have passed away and all things have become new. Do you accept forgiveness, Mary?" Jesus' voice was passionate, yet insistent.

Mary looked into his deep brown eyes and felt it in her spirit. She had been brought to a precipice and faced with a choice: she could either take the leap and soar, or back down and never know the rush of freedom he offered her. She hesitated. "But I am still Mary Magdalene!" she cried out in frustration and bitterness.

"You shall be called by a new name that the mouth of the Lord will bestow!" Jesus said with excitement.

Mary knew he was referring to the afterlife he always talked about, but she needed something for now. This life. "But what about now?!" she asked in distress. "I am Mary NOW!"

"Now, Mary, we must redeem your name. We must redeem the time you have lost under Satan's curse."

"But how?" she asked him quietly.

"Follow me," Jesus said.

Chapter 20

"Look at us! We're filthy and hungry! What should we do first?" Jesus laughed to the group as they walked into Jerusalem.

Nothing more than a tired rumbling answered him so Jesus suggested, "How about we eat, then rest?"

"Lord, where will we stay and what will we eat? We have no more money!" Judas said, shaking an empty coin purse for affect.

Mary's ears perked up. She felt a boldness strengthen her as she stepped forward and said to Jesus, "I do."

Both men looked at her, one in derision, and the other in love. Judas began to protest violently, but Jesus kept his eyes on Mary, reassuring her with his gaze that she was not out of line. Like he was just waiting for her to continue.

Refusing to look at the display Judas was making next to them, Mary kept her eyes on Jesus. Judas was spewing malicious things, condemning her for everyone to hear, mocking her offer and exposing again her shame. The men and women around them looked from him to Mary to Jesus with bewilderment. Jesus' eyes never left Mary.

Finally, Mary found the courage to continue. "I don't even know why I brought it."

"For this reason," Jesus said simply.

Mary was shocked by his implication. That all the money she brought was with a purpose, for Jesus, was mind blowing. And relieving. And such a tremendous blessing, if what he said was true. That the money from the sins of her past was covered under the atonement that made her clean before him. That she now had a significant gift to give him. Her money was now his, and would fund his ministry!

She smiled at Jesus, joy radiating from her face. "It's yours."

Jesus smiled back. "I accept it. Thank you, Mary."

Taking the bag from his shoulder, Jesus hoisted it onto Judas'.

"Judas, will you take care of this please? It's for the ministry."

Judas' jaw dropped as he took in the full weight of the bag Jesus handed him.

Jesus motioned for another man who was carrying the second bag, and he sent them both off ahead of the group to find lodging. Taking a few coins, Jesus led the rest of them through the market, then to a garden near the edge of town. They spread out to eat under a large Juniper.

"They'll find us here. It's my favorite place," Jesus said, smiling.

They ate in relative silence, after which Jesus left them to walk farther into the garden. Mary soon lost sight of him and felt very alone.

"May I join you?" Levi stood awkwardly, waiting for an answer from Mary. She nodded, then looked around self-consciously at the others to gauge their reactions. Most were too engrossed in their food or in conversations to notice. Only two or three were looking at Mary and Levi, and more with inquisitiveness than concern or condemnation. Mary smiled in gratification when they each smiled at her.

"You don't know most of these people, do you?" Levi asked. Without waiting for an answer, he stood up and said loudly to the group, "I realize most of us have been together a while and gotten to know one another, but my friend Mary here doesn't know hardly anyone. How about we introduce ourselves?"

He looked at Mary and winked, then sat down as the group moved in toward them.

"I'm sorry, Mary. How rude of us! I'm Salome. Of course, you and I have already met," she admitted sheepishly.

Mary smiled through the shock wave that immediately hit her. Was this the same woman who had verbally attacked her when they first met? Now her eyes were kind and Mary could see that she was being genuine.

It was such a relief to hear Salome continue. "Now, we meet as friends."

Mary smiled appreciatively and allowed Salome to squeeze her hand in a gesture of affection.

"I'm Peter," offered a tall gentleman behind her. She turned and smiled at him, taking his outstretched hand.

"Hello, Peter. It's so nice to meet you," Mary said congenially.

"This's my brother Andrew," he said, motioning to a younger man sitting across from them. Mary turned and gave a small wave to Andrew, who smiled and returned the gesture.

Before long, Mary felt surrounded by a group of friends. She repeated their names over and over to herself so she wouldn't forget them. James and John she knew she would remember. They looked so similar, Mary was sure they could be twins. Bartholomew would be easy to remember; he was the eldest among them. A few names danced around in her head, and she knew she'd have to ask Levi for help in remembering who Simon, Thaddeus and Thomas were. The women would be easier to remember because, besides herself, there was only Salome and Joanna, and another Mary.

Once they were all acquainted, the conversation flowed so smoothly among the whole group that Mary stopped noticing the passing time. She did notice, however, how things were changing. With these people and in herself.

They were all beginning to accept her and make her feel welcome, and she was letting herself be drawn into their circle. Mary hardly knew how to express her gratitude. The more they accepted and loved her, the less judgment she felt over her past. In fact, her past was losing its grip on her more and more as these wonderful people allowed her to move away from it and truly be free.

It seemed like no time at all before Judas and the man she learned was Phillip returned and showed the group where they would all be staying the night. The men spread out into five rooms on the first floor of the Inn and the women took two rooms on the second. Sleep greeted them at the door.

Chapter 21

Mary spent the next few days in the company of the women. The men were gone early the first morning and had not yet come back. In the meantime, the women had drawn massive amounts of water from the well and washed the piles of clothing the men had left behind, as well as their own.

Mary and Salome had walked to the market and purchased food on the first day, but since the men had not returned as expected, they now worried that it would go bad. Joanna suggested they share it with the men and women begging at the gates of the city, so they bundled up the large quantity of food they had expected to feed the men with and took it to the edge of the city.

Mary was surprised to see so many people there. Most of them wore little more than rags. Some had various appendages wrapped heavily or simply missing. Several were obviously blind. These responded with a blank, unfocused stare and mostly toothless grins when the women addressed them.

Mary wondered how Jesus would approach these people, and suddenly found that her heart was going out to them.

Their need penetrated her heart. She bent down and touched an older woman, smiling as she handed her some food.

Mary fed as many as she could with the portion of food she had brought, then sat talking to them, or rather listening, as they ate and shared their stories.

Looking fixedly off into the distance, Mary caught sight of a ragged group of people meandering on the plain. She could faintly detect their voices. Straining to hear what they were saying, she finally heard, "Unclean! Unclean!"

Mary sat up very straight, looking past the lepers to another group that was approaching them. These men seemed familiar and it did not take her long to realize it was Jesus and the others. They were approaching the lepers!

Scrambling to her feet, Mary hollered to them, hoping they would hear her above the nearer shouts of the lepers. Waving her arms violently, Mary ignored everyone around her who could not understand her sudden outburst.

She took off running in Jesus' direction, waving her arms and shouting at the top of her lungs. How could Jesus not know the customs regarding lepers? Didn't he understand the deadly disease ravaging their bodies, and how quickly it would spread through his own?

Suddenly, she stopped in horror. Jesus had touched one. Then another. A third threw himself at Jesus, wrapping his arms around his neck and weeping all over him.

Mary recoiled. She moaned and sank to the ground in agonizing fear. Jesus was now untouchable! She curled up over her lap.

"Oh God, no!" she screamed.

A thunderous noise drowned out Mary's cries. She looked up in horror to see the leprous men running toward, then past her.

She screamed and threw herself backward. They were laughing! Jumping, shouting and laughing! And running straight toward the city gate!

Mary watched them go, then stood quickly and brushed herself off as Jesus walked toward her. He was smiling and reached out to her. She reached out for his hand, then pulled back sharply.

Jesus' eyes penetrated her thoughts, and he could see that she was uncertain of him now because he had touched the lepers. He withheld his judgment and his reaction. His attention was immediately averted by the loud whooping shouts of joy coming from a man running toward him.

The man fell at his feet weeping, shouting out a jubilant praise and kissing Jesus' feet. Jesus laughed. "Stand up," he said, lifting the man to his feet.

"Weren't there ten of you? Where are the other nine? Has no one else come to give praise to God?"

The man wept and shook his head. Finally, he looked up expectantly at Jesus.

"Rise and go; your faith has made you well," Jesus assured him.

"Mary," Jesus said, kneeling down beside her. "The Lord has anointed me to preach good news to the poor. He sent me to bind up the broken hearted, to set captives free and to release those bound by demons. To comfort all who mourn and bestow on them a crown of beauty instead of ashes, the oil of joy instead of mourning and a garment of praise instead of a spirit of despair. I cannot withhold myself from them. "

"But their disease, Jesus… it's so contagious!" Mary said with great fear and concern.

Jesus looked at her in love. "The prince of this world has nothing in me."

He helped her to her feet and smiled. "It is for this that I have come into the world!"

Mary gave a faint smile in response, marveling at his passion and determination. She was finally getting used to the weird things he said, because she knew that no matter how strange it was, it was true. That meant something.

"We're headed to the synagogue. Would you ladies care to join us?"

"Jesus!" croaked a voice.

Mary looked down to see a man reaching out aimlessly as they passed by. Jesus turned and knelt beside him. "It's me," he said to the man as he took his hand and guided it to his lap.

"Lord, I want to see."

Judas came up behind him and crossed his arms. "Rabbi, who sinned, this man or his parents, that he was born blind?"

Jesus kept his eyes on the unseeing man as he spoke, "Neither this man nor his parents sinned. This happened so that the works of God might be displayed in him."

Jesus turned and spit on the ground next to the man's feet, then he rubbed it into the dirt, creating a mud paste. He gathered it up on his fingers and gently wiped it onto the man's eyes. "Go, wash in the pool of Siloam."

One of the others led the man away, and the rest of the group followed them into the city. Near the pool of Siloam was another, the pool of Bethesda, and there were many people laying on mats around the pool. This was the custom, Mary knew, for invalids with no one to take care of them. Or those just too desperate to go home.

Mary knew the superstitions: it was believed that an angel came down and stirred the water from time to time. It was said that the first person into the pool after the water was stirred was miraculously healed.

Mary had not been to Jerusalem since she was a child. She had never witnessed the truth or error in this belief. The sheer number of sick and dying around the pool quickly convinced her that, in the least, the waters were not stirred very often.

Walking near the outer edge of the disabled masses, Jesus stopped next to a mangled elderly man on a ragged mat. He looked down and asked, "What is your name?"

A murmur arose around them, and not without their own numbers. Mary did not hear the old man's response, but she strained her ears to catch as much as she could.

"How long have you been here?" Jesus asked.

"Thirty-eight years."

Jesus wrinkled his brow. "Don't you want to be well?"

Mary's heart ached at the man's reaction to that question. Tears welled up in his eyes and toppled over the rims. "So desperately," he whispered. "But there's no one to help me into the pool when the water is stirred. I have crawled down there and waited for days, expecting it to happen at any moment. But when the cry goes up, and I begin to inch my way toward the edge to fall into the water, someone else goes down ahead of me."

The injustice sunk into Mary. She looked around at the other lame and disabled. They were all so desperate! And they were willing to do whatever it took to be healed, even if it meant cheating and stealing.

The old man's countenance broke her heart. He held Jesus' hand and wept. Finally, Jesus said, "Get up!"

The man looked at Jesus, his face showing the same bewildered look the others had. He began to dissent, but Jesus continued, "Pick up your mat and walk!"

Those who could see watched in amazement as the old man's twisted legs uncurled and straightened. A cry arose from many as his legs gained a complexion befitting the young and athletic. His skin color returned instantly and he jumped up, surprised by the instant change in his body. He laughed. He cried. He shouted. Those around him stared in wonder. He reached and cupped the sides of Mary's face, kissed her forehead and laughed boisterously.

Joy spread like an infection among the others until they were all talking excitedly and laughing. Bending his new legs, the man rolled up his mat. At that moment, a booming voice demanded, "The law forbids this!"

A large, round man with a red face and an elaborate tunic stormed toward them. Mary knew immediately he was a Pharisee. His garment hung with tassels, and his beard and hair were trimmed in the usual fashion. Within seconds, he was in front of the man who had just been healed, screaming in rage. "You cannot carry your mat on the Sabbath! Put it down!"

He stomped his foot and pointed forcefully at the ground. The healed paralytic looked at him in confusion and said, "The man who made me well said to me, 'Pick up your mat and walk.'"

The Pharisee looked around and asked vehemently, "Who is this man who told you to pick it up and walk?"

Mary's eyes scanned the crowd with the rest of them, looking for Jesus. He was nowhere to be seen.

"I ... I don't know who he was. He just asked me if I wanted to be well and told me to get up, pick up my mat and walk. And look," he said, getting excited again and throwing his arms out to fully display his new ability, "I am walking!"

The Pharisee rebuked him harshly then turned and stormed away. The man began looking around again. Recognizing Mary, he asked, "You were with him ... do you know where he went?"

"He was headed to the temple," she whispered.

"I must thank him!"

The man turned and excitedly walked through hundreds of others lying around on mats in various stages of physical torment. He waved and shouted in triumphant joy about his healing.

Cries came from everywhere, wondering at his healing and imploring him to bring the healer back. Mary watched sadly as men and women dragged themselves toward the pool under the assumption that a mysterious visitation would soon happen. So many people were longing for a healing.

****

An awful uproar greeted them as they approached the temple. Mary pushed through a mob of curious spectators so she could see better, and there, in the midst of the indoor market that always preceded Passover, an angry Jesus with a whip in his hand was swinging it violently at animals and men alike and yelling at the top of his lungs.

"Get out! Get these animals out of here! It is written 'My house shall be called a house of prayer,' but you have made it a den of robbers. Get out!"

Mary watched in horror as he clutched the side of a table covered in money and tossed it away, scattering the coins and scaring the men behind it. The merchants and moneychangers ran indiscriminately toward the gaping crowd.

Jesus broke open the dove cage and birds flew everywhere. He then turned to the sheep pen and released them. Bleating sheep ran in every direction in panic as Jesus released the cattle in the next pen.

The mesmerized crowd broke up quickly, fleeing in all directions as the cows and sheep came flying at them en mass. Hiding behind a large pillar to avoid the fleeing animals, Mary listened to the indignant cries of Jesus as he cleared the temple.

The shouting persisted for a while, then died down. Mary finally found the courage to continue up the steps toward the outer court. The paralyzed man was nowhere to be seen.

She found Jesus in the midst of a large gathering of people. He was calmly listening to them, touching them, healing them and hugging them. She could hear the tenderness in his voice as he conversed with them. She was close enough to see the pain in his face that reflected the years of torment each one related to him. Occasionally, she could see a tear slide down his cheek.

She watched the children come up to him and throw their arms around his neck. He would laugh and hug them back fiercely. He would kiss their cheeks and send them off to hug or heal the next person. She loved watching him with people. He was so comfortable. And he radiated love to each one of them. Individually.

Mary saw the man who had come with her to the temple. Timidly approaching Jesus, he thanked Jesus for healing him and said excitedly, "I even walked all the way here!" He showed Jesus that he could now jump and dance, and Jesus laughed in joy at the demonstration.

"See, you are well again," Jesus said. "Stop sinning or something worse will happen to you," he warned.

The man shook his head in solemn agreement, then walked away with a wide smile.

Jesus continued touching and healing those around him. Within hours, the temple court was scattered with abandoned mats. Hundreds of men and women walked the streets of Jerusalem without the aid of another person. Many others beheld their families for the first time in many years, if not in their whole lifetime. Still others heard the rowdy market and the laughter of children for the first time. In one accord, the majority of Jerusalem's inhabitants sang praises to God for the wonderful things he had done.

Chapter 22

Very early the next morning, a rapid knock on the door woke Mary. Wrapping her shawl around herself, she peeked out to see Levi standing there anxiously. The familiarity of greeting him this way brought a sudden wave of nausea, and Mary briefly lost her composure. The urgency in his voice brought her back.

"Mary, wake the others. We are leaving to go back to Bethany."

"Is something the matter?" she asked, immediately concerned.

"Wake the others. I will explain on the way. Hurry Mary!" he urged quietly before turning away.

Mary woke the others and before long, their things were packed and they met the men on the road outside the inn. Mary found Levi and asked excitedly, "What is it?" Then she saw Jesus walk past her quickly. Her heart dropped. His head was bent and she heard distinctly the sound of heaving sobs.

"What's happened?" She whispered in alarm.

"It's Lazarus," Levi said, choking up. "He's … he's dead."

"No!" Mary whispered. Her hand flew instinctively up to her mouth as a cry of anguish burst forth.

Levi put his arms around Mary's shoulder to comfort her and coax her on as the group hastily caught up with Jesus.

"What happened?" Mary asked in despair.

"A man came to us the day after we got here and said Lazarus was sick. Jesus was teaching in the temple, and I saw him get choked up, but then he looked at us and assured us, 'This sickness will not end in death. It is for God's glory, so that God's son may be glorified through it.' So we prayed together for Lazarus' healing and then thought nothing else of it. There were so many around us who needed ministered to, we fell back into the work and put our concerns out of our minds. We trusted his word.

"Last night, he left us to go pray. He was in such deep distress, but he didn't tell any of us why. He was gone all night! He came this morning and woke us up, insisting we go back to Bethany. Of course, everyone protested. They just recently tried to stone him there!" Mary did not know this, and a sudden fear engulfed her. She bit her nails to keep from interrupting Levi.

"He told us, 'Our friend Lazarus has fallen asleep; but I am going to wake him up.' Someone threw a pillow at him and laughed. Peter said, 'Duh!' Weren't we all just sleeping? Why's it so important to go wake him up now?' Then Thomas said, 'Lord, if he sleeps he will get better.'" A cry stuck in Levi's throat as he finished, "That when Jesus told us plainly that Lazarus had died."

Bethany was not far from Jerusalem, and before long, Mary could hear the sounds of the town waking up. She was surprised to hear Martha's voice coming nearer. Rushing to the front of the procession, Mary watched as Martha clung to Jesus, crying. "Lord, if you had been here, my brother would not have died!"

Jesus pulled her into his arms and held her as she sobbed. She lifted her face to him and implored, "I know even now God will give you whatever you ask."

Jesus looked at her affectionately and said, "Your brother will rise again." The words came out calmly, and Mary felt that familiar peace penetrate the atmosphere around them.

"I know he will rise again in the resurrection at the last day," Martha said. She closed her eyes and breathed in the peace.

Jesus looked off into the distance and said, "I am the resurrection and the life. The one who believes in me will live, even though they die; and whoever lives by believing in me will never die. Do you believe this?" he asked her gently.

"Yes, Lord," she replied. Her eyes still closed, she clung even tighter to him. "I believe that you are the Messiah, the Son of God, who is to come into the world."

Martha's arms fell and she turned away to walk back toward her house alone. Mary could not persuade herself to follow Martha. Decorum was lost as she stood motionless, transfixed on Jesus. He was agonizingly weeping. His arms were raised to the sky and they could hear him crying out to God.

Suddenly, a swarm of people rushed to them, led by the younger sister, Mary. She fell at Jesus' feet and cried out in deep anguish, "Lord, if you had been here, my brother would not have died!"

Jesus looked down at her with such compassion even though his own heart was being torn in two. "Where have you laid him?"

"Come and see," someone said.

Jesus bent down and pulled Mary up to her feet. He wrapped his arms around her and cried with her.

"See how much he loved him?" Levi whispered.

Mary watched, engrossed in the intimate way he grieved with the young woman. She overheard someone else ask, "Couldn't he who opened the eyes of the blind man have kept this man from dying?"

They followed the mourners away from the village to a small tomb cut out of the side of a hill. There was a large, flat stone blocking the entrance to the tomb. Mary was surprised when Jesus said, "Take away the stone."

Martha face turned white with horror. "But Lord, he's been there four days," she gasped.

"Didn't I tell you that if you believe, you will see the glory of God? Take the stone away."

Several men worked together to remove the stone. Lifting his face to the sky, Jesus prayed loudly, "Father, I thank you that you have heard me. I know that you always hear me, but I said this for the benefit of the people standing here, that they may believe that you sent me."

Lowering his head to look directly into the tomb, Jesus said in a loud, commanding voice, "Lazarus, come out!"

Mary's mouth fell open as a literal motion of surprise moved across the hillside. Cries and praises came from every direction as a fully wrapped body filled the doorway of the tomb.

Beside her, the younger Mary fainted into Peter, whose shock turned into laughter. He caught her, but stumbled and fell beneath her weight. There he sat, laughing and praising God, holding Mary.

The hillside erupted. Some laughed, some cried, many still wailed. Jesus held Martha as she cried in joy. Mary Magdalene sank to the ground, overwhelmed by the miracle before her. Though tears streamed down her face, she was so full of joy and admiration, laughter was spilling out unbidden. Mary was intoxicated.

Jesus gestured in the general direction of his disciples and said, "Take off his grave clothes so he can go home!"

Levi joined a few others in unwrapping Lazarus, who stood there in awe at the revival around him. Rushing to her brother, Martha threw her arms around him. Another of the mourners threw a cloak around him.

Jesus lifted his arms up to the heavens and praised his father. For hours, the hills were alive with the sounds of worship and prayer. Mary's heart swelled with joy and pride. Look what her Lord had done!

Lazarus was not cripple, blind, deaf or demon possessed. He was dead. And Jesus had not even prayed over him or about him. He had simply spoken to God in appreciation for His presence, and then spoken a word to Lazarus. "Come forth!" And Lazarus had walked out of the tomb! Could there be any greater miracle than this?

Chapter 23

After several days with Lazarus, Jesus revealed his plans to go to Nazareth to retrieve his family for the Passover. By this time, their numbers had dwindled again to include a handful of men and women who always accompanied Jesus. They decided with one accord that they would go with him. Even Lazarus and his sisters. Mary was delighted to spend the next few days with Martha. She helped the women pack a few things and prepare a final breakfast before they left.

Soon, they were on the road again, walking at a leisurely pace. Mary kept company with the women, delighted that they all were treating her like she belonged, and she finally felt like she did. The burden of her past had become a distant memory among these men and women she had grown to love.

Their small gang took on more and more people as they journeyed through Bethel and Shiloh. Many approached Jesus for healing. Others sat on the roadside yelling for him. He touched them all. In return, some followed him. Most went back to their homes and families, happy to be set free from the torment of illness or demonic possession.

The women slowly gave away all their food and meager belongings to those who were in need. Jesus reached into the bag Judas held covetously, and gave each of them a handful of money to disperse to the men and women who approached them. Several times, he did this and his disciples gave very liberally to anyone who expressed a need.

The gang traveled this way for five days, sleeping along the roads at night and waking with the sun. It was a slow progression because of the many who came to Jesus. He did not turn anyone away. He healed, comforted, kissed and embraced every person who showed up in need.

Mary was astonished at the constant flow of the needy that flocked to him. And even more astonished at his untiring reception of them. Never faltering or flagging in his acceptance, Jesus gave his all to each person, yet never was empty. He seemed perpetually equipped to handle the sea of humanity that grappled for his attention. It was amazing.

When they reached Nazareth at last, Jesus expressed his own need: to be left alone when he went home to get his mother. The group eagerly agreed.

While they discussed among themselves where to go for a decent meal and rest, Jesus pulled Mary Magdalene aside. "I would like for you to come with me," he said timidly.

Mary was astounded. "Sure," she said, wondering at his invitation.

"I want you to meet my mother," Jesus said with a smile.

Together, they parted from the group and walked into a sleepy Nazareth. They stopped at an unassuming house in the middle of town, not far from the local cistern. "I played in that thing every day," Jesus laughed. "And got scolded every day."

Mary laughed at the thought of Jesus as a rambunctious boy. "I'll bet you drove your mother crazy," she teased him.

"Oh quite!" he laughed. "I'm taking you to meet her. My crazy mother who once was sane." He laughed again, then knocked on the door.

Mary was surprised when a young woman answered the door. "Jesus!" she screeched, then threw her arms around his neck and kissed his cheek. He returned her affections, then introduced her to Mary, "My sister, Ruth."

Ruth smiled at Mary, still clasping Jesus' hand and pulled him into the room. "Mother, Jesus is here!"

Several young men bounded into the room and tackled Jesus en mass. He fell to the floor laughing and fighting off the playful blows from his brothers. Their banter continued until an older woman walked into the room.

"Take this nonsense outside!" she insisted. Her eyes found Mary and she smiled wide.

The mound of men on the floor stopped squirming and separated to reveal five distinct bodies. Jesus stood and helped the others to their feet one by one, introducing them. "This is Joseph. This," he grunted, pulling a resisting brother to his feet, "is James … My brother, Judas. And," another grunt and laughter, "this one is Simon."

"A girl!" Simon teased, to which Jesus replied with a punch to the arm. Mary's face turned red, and she lowered her eyes in embarrassment.

"A woman," corrected Jesus' mother as she approached Mary and embraced her tenderly.

"This is Mary," Jesus said to the room. "She's a friend of mine and I wanted her to meet you." He smiled at her, then said to his mother, "Especially you, Mother."

His mother smiled and led Mary into the next room, which was the kitchen. She pulled out a chair for Mary, then busied herself making tea for them.

"It's not every day Jesus brings a woman home," his mother said with a twinkle in her eye.

Jesus stood at the doorway and smiled at his mother. "It's not exactly what you think, Mother."

His mother gave him a look of disappointment and rebuke. To Mary she said, "You can call me Mother."

Mary smiled and offered a small "thank you" before dropping her gaze to the table to avoid the awkwardness of Mary's assumptions and Jesus' correction. Her stomach tied in knots at the invitation to call Jesus' mother "mother." She had not used that word to address anyone since her own mother passed away, and of all people, she expected that Jesus' mother would instinctively discern her shame and treat her just like Salome had. She was shocked and comforted by this genuine acceptance.

Jesus' mother's preparations seemed to become louder and more agitated after this. Finally, she sat down, having prepared and served tea to Mary, Jesus and herself.

"What is it, Son?" she asked, obviously annoyed that he was not introducing this woman as a love interest.

"Mother!" Jesus rebuked her gently, laughing.

"I'm sorry! I just don't understand why you keep doing this to me! You bring them in or take me to them, and yet none of them are here to stay!"

Jesus looked down at his hands, letting silence invade their circle. Then he looked up at his mother with moist eyes and said, "Mother, we've discussed this. You know why."

His short statement brought tears to his mother's eyes. She looked down and wiped them away. Glancing up at her son, she nodded her head. Though she said nothing, she seemed to convey so much to him.

Mary could see Jesus' mother had a longing, and was puzzled at the exchange between them. What did it mean? She watched, feeling like a fly on the wall. Within the silence was such an intimate conversation, she felt like she was intruding. Sipping her tea, Mary did her best to distract herself.

After an uncomfortable silence, Jesus said, "Passover is almost here. We came to help you get ready to go to Jerusalem."

Looking lovingly at her eldest son, the older Mary patted his hand. "Of course. Thank you."

"We need to leave tomorrow. Will you be ready by then?"

"There's a lot to do," his mother mused.

"Mary and I will stay and help. I will rally the boys and Mary can help you and Ruth pack your things."

Jesus looked at Mary for approval and she nodded in agreement to the plan. His mother smiled at her again, and thanked them both. Then she stood, took Jesus' cup of tea and flung its contents out the window.

"Hey!" Jesus laughed. "What'd you do that for?"

His mother returned to the table and sat down with a stubborn look on her face. "You're dismissed. We women have a lot to talk about."

Jesus laughed again and left the kitchen. Mary was instantly full of dread. She had been left alone with Jesus' mother and felt unprotected and vulnerable. She smiled, trying to cover her angst. His mother, Mary, smiled back.

"How are you, Mary?" she asked.

Mary found her very likable, and soon the two were absorbed in general conversation about what preparations needed to be made so they could leave the next day. Mary then set about the kitchen, cleaning things and preparing food while Jesus' mother went to induce her brood to action.

Soon, the house was buzzing with activity. Everyone but Jesus stopped by the kitchen intermittently to observe the lovely stranger among them. Mary would notice someone or another watching, and smile as they instantly disappeared into another room.

Eventually, she moved into the common room in the front and began tidying up there. She still had not seen Jesus since he left the kitchen. Finally, he poked his head through the front door. "You doing okay?"

Mary smiled and nodded. Jesus smiled back and said, "Do you mind if I ..." He hesitated then went on, "I ... my mother has invited us to stay the night."

Mary smiled and said, "That's nice."

"You wouldn't mind staying here?"

"No, I guess that wouldn't be so bad. We're all going together in the morning?"

"Yes ... Mary?" Jesus cleared his throat. "I, uh ... I won't be staying."

Mary was both relieved and disappointed. She was relieved that his family's assumptions would quickly be laid to rest. But disappointed because now she would be staying in a house full of strangers without anyone familiar. She recovered quickly, hoping he didn't know what was going on inside her. "That'll be okay," she lied, and looked back to the work she was doing before he interrupted her attention.

Jesus came in and stood next to her. "It will be okay," he said, lifting her face to look at him.

Mary bit her lip and smiled, defying the emotions going on inside her. She recognized a slew of emotions on Jesus' face and looked away quickly to avoid seeing them. Rather than being pleased that he was bothered on her behalf, Mary was ashamed. Jesus was the only man to not want something from her, and she needed that. The last thing she wanted was for Jesus to have any feelings whatsoever for her.

Simon and Joseph rushed into the room, pushing each other playfully and creating a sudden racket that distracted Mary and Jesus enough to break up their emotional tryst. Mary turned back to her work and Jesus chased his brothers out the front door and down the road.

Chapter 24

Mary found Jesus' mother sitting in the same chair, holding the same cup of cold tea she was cradling the night before when Mary turned in. Her white knuckles betrayed the fact that she had been holding the cup for hours in stricken terror. Mary rushed to her.

"What is it, Mother?"

The older woman looked up into Mary's concerned face and said with dread, "The last time I went to Jerusalem with Jesus, they tried to stone him." Her face was ashen, her eyes full of fear.

Mary did not know this. She had never seen anyone react to Jesus in any way but awe. Except for the Pharisees, who strongly disapproved of him healing a man on the Sabbath. But she had mostly been involved with Jesus in much smaller groups. She could easily see a larger group getting out of hand.

Jesus' mother bent her head down to the table and began to weep. Wrapping her arms around the older woman's shoulders, Mary held her and prayed that the comfort she wished to give would saturate this incredible woman. She didn't know what to say, or how to console her in the least. So she just held her tight while the elder Mary fell to pieces.

It didn't take long for the others in the house to wake up. Ruth rushed into the kitchen and asked with alarm, "What's wrong with my mother?"

She moved in to hug her, and Mary moved so that she could, backing up against a counter and folding her arms across herself. Simon and James came into the room next. "What's going on?" James asked, defensively.

Raising her head, their mother did her best to console them in her grief. "I'm alright, children. I'm all right. Let's all finish preparing to go to Jerusalem –" Her voice broke off and she shook with the sorrow that overcame her.

"Mother, he'll be alright. He'll be alright. Or he wouldn't be taking us ... right?" Ruth whispered to her mother.

Slipping out of the kitchen, Mary headed for the front door. She needed air and a quiet place to think. When she opened the door, Jesus stood there with his friend John and Martha.

"Hey!" Jesus said emphatically.

Quickly recognizing the confusion and fear on her face, Jesus asked, "What's wrong?"

Mary shook her head as tears filled her eyes. Sidestepping the others, she walked to the road. Jesus followed her. "Is everything ok? Did you have a bad night here?"

"No, everything's fine," she said. Jesus tugged her arm until they were facing each other, then searched Mary's eyes. The tenderness of his gaze pressed her into confession.

"Everything's not fine. Your mom is near hysterics in there. She said you were nearly stoned the last time she went to Jerusalem with you. Is that true?" Her voice pleaded with him. It broke his heart. Swallowing hard, Jesus admitted, "Yes."

Mary was flabbergasted. She wanted him to tell her more, but he offered no explanation. He turned toward Martha and John. "Can you guys get them ready and meet us on the road? I need to talk to Mary."

Martha and John both nodded, and Martha shot Mary a smile before they walked into the house. Jesus turned toward the northern road, his head bent in concentration. Mary followed him.

"You haven't known me very long, and there's a lot you've missed that might surprise you. For instance, I'm not really that popular."

An involuntarily chuckle escaped Jesus, which further confused Mary. Was he being serious?

Jesus was completely serious. Dropping her eyes to the road again, Mary waited for the rest of this new revelation from this man who had come to mean so much to her.

"Many people come to me for healings, and many follow me to see what I have to say. But there are few who stay with me because they love me. Like you," he said, smiling down at her.

"And of course, there are many who hate me because I testify that the deeds they do are evil. And I must. Because my teachings are not my own. Everything that I say and do comes from the one who sent me."

Searching the horizon for meaning, Jesus waited for Mary to react. She tried to arrange all the things she knew about him in her mind so it made a cohesive statement about who he was, but she still was not sure she completely understood. Jesus sensed this and went on.

"You are of this world. I am not of this world." He paused for a few seconds then tried a different route. "Do you remember the dragon, Mary?"

She nodded her head, and he continued, though now his voice seemed impatient and emotional. "Remember how I told you that I am the one spoken of in the prophecies that would destroy the dragon and his work?" She nodded again.

Jesus stopped and turned Mary to him. He held her at arms' length and said, "Do you know the scriptures, Mary? Do you know that the wages of sin is death?"

Mary had never heard these scriptures before. Jesus was looking at her fiercely. Sweat dotted his forehead. Panic pushed the words out fast as he spoke. "Satan demanded a ransom for the souls of mankind. There is no other way! It's the reason I was sent here. The reason I preach tirelessly all over the region. The reason I can't sleep or eat. The reason I battle the desire to be normal and have a normal life, to pursue you, Mary. To marry someone and finally make my mom happy. Because I will give my life as a ransom for many!"

The truth dawned on her. The puzzling pieces she had gathered and put together finally created a whole, awful truth she had to face: Jesus was going to die.

Mary was stunned. Jesus raised his face to the sky and closed his eyes. She watched him drink peace from the heavens. Before she could ask him why he didn't run from it, how he could so willingly lay down and die, he answered her as if she had spoken the question out loud. "It is better that one man die for the people than all the nations perish."

Mary could see that he had made up his mind. That he would go through with it, in spite of anyone's feelings about it. There was a cause in him she hardly understood, but he was resolutely set on defeating the enemy of mankind. Of slaying the dragon and setting captives free. She was as proud of him as she was terrified by the enormous death-cloud lingering over them.

Jesus took her hand and turned them back toward Jerusalem. "Will you stay with me, Mary? Will you walk this road with me to the end?'"

This time, it was his eyes that pleaded with her. Mary looked up at him with such love. "Where you go, I will go."

Chapter 25

The walk back toward Jerusalem was a quiet several days. Martha prodded Mary for details, teasing her about her sudden popularity with Jesus. Mary shrugged off her suggestions and insisted they were just friends. It was hard for her to engage in conversation with the weight of his revelation pressing on her heart, so she remained quiet most of the way back.

They lodged at various inns along the way, maintaining a slow pace for the sake of Jesus' mother. Within five days, they were back in Bethany at Lazarus' house. Martha dragged Mary into the kitchen and the two set about preparing dinner for the whole tired crew. Meanwhile, Jesus and a few other men rearranged the living room into a makeshift dining hall to accommodate their large group. By evening time, they were all settled in. After the women arranged dinner on the table, they sat down to eat with the men.

As they were finishing up their meal, Lazarus' sister Mary entered the room. No one had noticed her missing until they all looked up to see her standing beside Jesus with tears streaming down her cheeks. She held a bottle in her hands, which she delicately unscrewed and tilted over his head. Martha gasped, seeing it was the perfume her father bought her before he died. Her sister had never opened it.

Jesus closed his eyes and sat very still as the oil flowed down his head and hair, onto his shoulders and down his arms and chest. No one else in the room moved. The entire house was instantly filled with the beautiful fragrance.

Abruptly, Judas stood and pointed an accusing finger at her. "That perfume was worth a year's wages," he said disdainfully. "Why wasn't it sold and given to the poor?"

Jesus' eyes flew open. "Leave her alone!" he commanded. "It was intended that she should save this perfume for the day of my burial. She has done a good thing."

The young woman crumpled at Jesus' feet and wept. Mary's heart went out to her. Hadn't she also experienced this blessed compulsion to anoint the Savior's feet?

Jesus closed his eyes and began to pray, resting one hand on Lazarus' sister's trembling body and raising the other as if to touch the face of God. He spoke in an unknown language, which might have confused the others had peace not drawn them into prayer with him.

Mary felt her body push everything in her out of her mouth in prayer to God. She was overwhelmed with gratitude and joy. It was like a spring coming out of the depths of her soul.

The unified prayer ebbed and flowed harmoniously for an undetermined amount of time. When Mary was finished praising God, she opened her eyes and was surprised to see the house filled up with people. The entire town had come to see Jesus and Lazarus.

After several hours, the women cleared the table and wandered into the adjoining rooms to sleep while the men talked the night away in the other room. By morning, most of them were gone, including Jesus.

****

"Blessed is he who comes in the name of the Lord!"
"Hosanna! Hosanna to the Son of David!"
"Blessed is the king of Israel!"
"Peace! Peace in heaven and glory in the highest!"

Mary's heart leapt within her. She was surrounded by a loud, exalting crowd and it was euphoric! They were making their way down the Mount of Olives toward the city and spontaneous praise erupted from the lips of those that had gathered to witness Jesus' coming into Jerusalem.

The disciples had seated him on a colt, and people were throwing their outer-garments and shawls on the ground to carpet the road before him. Men were hacking palm branches and handing them to women, who were waving them in exultation toward him. Children were dancing in the street and singing out at the tops of their lungs.

A man pushed past Mary to the front of the throng. His arrogant swagger and familiar tassels instantly identified him as a Pharisee. He charged in front of the donkey and commanded, "Teacher, rebuke your disciples!"

The donkey kept moving forward, completely dismissing the enraged man. Jesus looked down and replied calmly, "I tell you, if they keep quiet, the stones will cry out."

Several other men rushed towards Jesus and demanded he silence the crowd and send them home. But Jesus' face was set like flint. He refused to acknowledge their demands. The deluge pressed past the dumbstruck Pharisees and on toward Jerusalem, forcefully advancing by the reverie of the masses and the determination of their king.

The multitude in Jerusalem was much thicker. The sea of humanity had swelled there in anticipation of Passover. The temple was packed and the makeshift market within was in full swing.

Mary turned anxiously to see Jesus' reaction to the temple swarm. His face was stern and angry. He rushed into the temple portico and threw over the moneychanger's table. Onlookers were stunned by his audacity, and the merchants were appalled. Men came from every direction to try to restrain Jesus, but he easily pushed past them and opened cages and pens to release the animals brought in for profit.

Voices shouted, "NO! We need those!"

"What will people sacrifice?"

"How will they tithe with foreign money?"

"Those animals were bought with a price!"

Jesus did not care. He released every last one of them, without repentance. "This house is to be house of prayer. Not your money-maker!"

When he had thoroughly upset the men and women doing business in the church, he sat down and leaned back against a pillar. The people that had come into the city with him crept into the temple, wading past the men and women searching for coins and any trace of their livestock.

In no time, Jesus had drawn scores of people and his voice carried throughout the halls of the temple. Mary sat with Martha and the others, listening to the cadence of his voice as he taught them. She looked around to see how people were responding to him, and was surprised that there were few reactions among the laymen. They were all listening intently, their faces set on understanding.

Along the outer edges of the room stood the Pharisaical sect, their tunics displaying their knowledgeable edge above the rest. Their noses pointed resolutely toward the ceiling, and their eyebrows often followed suit. Many of them were rudely displaying their disagreements and general consternation of Jesus, snorting and chuckling as he talked, shaking their heads in disgust, and being otherwise incapable of the silence everyone else desired of them.

A small commotion next to Mary drew her attention, and she noticed Jesus' mother was crying quietly next to her.

"Mother, what's wrong?" she whispered.

The older Mary shook her head and silently waved Mary off. But her turmoil did not cease.

Mary gently offered to escort her out of the temple and away from the rabble. She was secretly full of her own anguish, because she had hoped to sit with the others for as long as Jesus taught and hear more from him. But this frail woman with an indescribable pain needed her more, so she grasped his mother's hand and led her through the labyrinth of people and out of the temple.

"Are you alright?" Mary asked the other.

Jesus' mother stood with tears streaming down her face. Her body was shaking uncontrollably, and Mary did not know how to comfort her.

"It is piercing me!" she shrieked out in anguish. Mary was bewildered.

"What is?" she asked, panicked.

The older Mary reached an arm toward heaven and pounded her chest with the other. "His sword is piercing me!"

Mary was incredulous. Who's sword? What was she talking about? Had Jesus' mother suddenly gone mad?!

The older Mary sank to the ground in agony and cried out in distress. Mary knelt beside her, clutching her shoulders. Her eyes darted from Mary to the people walking around them.

"Mother ... Mother, stand up," Mary coaxed gently.

After much effort, Jesus' mother stood, and Mary led her back to the safety of the garden of Gethsemane.

"I was just a girl then," the elder Mary whispered. The younger woman sat beside her and listened reverently as Jesus' mother poured out her heart.

"An angel came to me and told me I would conceive. I'd never even been with a man! He told me I'd have a son, and that he would be called the son of God. But we were to call him 'Jesus,'" she said tenderly.

The memory of a mother's first love was on her face as she spoke his name. Focusing again on Mary, she continued.

"The first visitation was strange enough. But then there was another. My Joseph had the same revelation. So our marriage started out under a shroud of shame neither one of us had any control over. All we knew was that ... we knew." She shrugged her shoulders as if that was all she had to cling to.

"So many things happened that confirmed God's leading, but the one I always remembered the most happened right here ... in this temple." She began to cry as she went on, "He was eight days old. My husband and I brought him here to dedicate him. There was an older gentleman in the temple, Simeon, who took him from me and began to go through the ceremonial prayers."

A fresh wave of anguish washed over her and she wept harder. "I will never forget his words," the diminutive elder said quietly. She read them off the scroll forever ingrained on her heart. "Sovereign Lord, as you have promised, you may now dismiss your servant in peace. For my eyes have seen your salvation, which you have prepared in the sight of all nations; a light for revelation to the Gentiles, and the glory of your people Israel."

The older woman sought understanding from Mary's eyes as she continued. "Then he looked right into my soul and said, 'This child is destined to cause the falling and rising of many in Israel, and to be a sign that will be spoken against, so that the thoughts of many hearts will be revealed.'"

The color drained from Jesus' mother's face as she went on. "And a sword will pierce your own soul too."

A fresh wave of grief washed over her and she burst out weeping bitterly. Cupping her face in her hands, Jesus' mother cried out in renewed agony.

"It is piercing me, Mary," she whispered through her anguished tears. "These people worship him with their lips, but their hearts are so far from him. They're going to kill my son!"

She clung to Mary as if clinging to a life raft. Her face showed the depth of despair in her heart. "My Jesus!" she cried. Burying her face in Mary's breast, she grieved for her first born.

Chapter 26

A heaviness in her chest was suffocating Mary, and she woke up fighting to remove the burden. She sat up and gulped air desperately. While everyone around her slept peacefully, another fitful night assured she was awake again before dawn.

The room was stifling hot and very claustrophobic. Pulling her clothing on and grabbing her shawl, she left the house as quietly as she knew how. Before she knew it, she was walking the road toward Jerusalem, more out of habit than purpose.

She walked quickly, trying to escape the dread she felt and soon, she was in the garden of Gethsemane. It was such a comforting place. Jesus had taken them there often. Between the moon and the hint of sun on the horizon, there was just enough light for Mary to see the outline of familiar rocks and trees.

Perching on a large boulder, Mary inhaled a deep breath of fresh air. She hugged her knees to her chest and closed her eyes, taking in large droughts of air to satisfy the emptiness in her chest.

"Mary."

Her eyes flew open and she jerked to see the person behind the voice. "Jesus! You frightened me!" she gasped.

"I'm sorry," he said, sincerely.

"What are you doing here?" Mary asked.

"I come to the garden alone often," Jesus told her. "It's peaceful here, and I needed to pray." Looking at her curiously, he asked, "What are you doing here?"

Mary looked up at the sky and sighed, "Waiting for the sun."

Jesus leaned against the rock she was sitting on. "Here I am," he said teasingly. Mary giggled and shoved his shoulder playfully. "Not you," she said. "That."

Pointing to the bright orange hue peeking out in the east, she explained, "It's my favorite time of day. It beckons me."

Jesus looked off toward the east and asked, "What do you find so captivating there?"

Mary pondered his question before answering. She felt like a little girl again, about to say something silly. She rested her cheek on her knees with her face toward him.

"All night long, darkness prevails. Until right now. The threat of light begins to rise in the east, and right before your eyes, darkness runs away and the sun rules the day."

She threw up her hands in celebration for the sun's victory. Jesus watched her with fascination. "Wow. That's deep."

Mary appreciated that he was not making fun of her. She had told him something so personal and he had taken her seriously.

"Jesus, can I tell you something?"

"Mm hmm," Jesus said.

"You've been talking about things lately that I find a little … unnerving," Mary said.

Jesus contemplated her words. "Me too," he said softly.

"I'm scared," Mary whimpered.

"Me too."

"Why do you keep saying you have to die?" Mary stammered.

Jesus shifted to face Mary. "God loves the world so much, Mary, that he sent me, his only son, to defeat Satan and offer eternal life to anyone who will believe in me," he explained. "When I die, my blood will become the sin offering that no offering before could satisfy. So deep is the need of mankind. So binding is the contract between man and Satan. I will die for you, Mary. And pay a ransom with my life, so that I can have you in eternity."

"Me?" Mary asked.

"As many as will believe in me."

"How can you do it?" Mary asked desperately.

The pain showed clearly on Jesus' face when he answered, "The spirit in me is willing, but the flesh is weak."

His voice broke under a potent wave of emotion. "I have prayed 'Father, if it's possible, let this cup pass from me.' I have agonized over it. I am struggling to carry this mantle my Father has placed on me. But imagine the victory, Mary."

Jesus' eyes were wide with an expression of joy. "Imagine when sin and death can no longer threaten the lives of God's people. Imagine freedom, Mary!" Jesus clasped her hands in his own. "I will give that to you."

She didn't know how to respond to him. She had no idea what to say. Those things sounded so wonderful. And so did having him forever. But the cost! Oh the cost!

"They're going to kill you?" she asked weakly.

"They are not taking my life. I am laying it down willingly," Jesus told her. "But I have the authority to take it back up again. And I will rise, Mary."

With nothing left to say, Jesus leaned into the rock Mary was perched on and together, they watched the sunrise. It was one of the only things Mary could always be certain of. The sunrise. Her life had always been so chaotic and unpredictable. The sunrise was often her only comfort. The only stability she knew. The sun would always rise. As she watched it next to him, Jesus' words echoed in her spirit, *"I will rise, Mary."*

Chapter 27

Emotions swelled over the next few days. A feverish debate raged in the temple between Jesus and the teachers of the law, with sea of humanity tossing helplessly between the two sides. The men and women closest to Jesus held on to their convictions, being resolutely on the side of Christ. The Pharisees and Sadducees became more determinedly against him. Vacillating between the two sides, swayed by the cunning of words on one side, and the witness of their spirits on the other, was all of Jerusalem and many thousands from the outlying regions of Israel.

Mary's mind ran through the events and conversations of the past week as she washed the evening dishes. She was standing in a stranger's kitchen among the other women who ministered to the needs of the group, but her heart and mind were miles away, wandering aimlessly among the terrain created by Jesus' words, seeking some comfort.

This new area created in her was dark and foreboding. Mary was terrified as she traversed it. The path of love had led her up a mountain of public opinion and shame, and she had enjoyed for a while the peak of peace and self-acceptance. But now, she was lost in a wilderness of doubt and fear, and she was terrified. She did not understand how Jesus could stand before them every day, exuding confidence and peace, while simultaneously preaching of his own betrayal, torture and death.

Mary replayed the events of the evening meal. For the first time in her life, she had celebrated the Passover with people she considered her family. She had anticipated it for weeks, and had mixed feelings now that it was over. It was the strangest ceremony she had ever experienced. It was beautiful and peaceful, but left her soul grieving.

In the most loving way, Jesus had begun the night by kneeling and washing the feet of everyone there. Most hosts provide water for guests to wash. Jesus had stooped before each one of them, a towel wrapped around his waist and a full basin in his hands. He had washed the dirt of the road off their feet. It was so humbling to be served in such a way, by a man so exalted in their hearts.

"No, Lord, you shall never wash my feet!" Peter had said, embarrassed by the situation. But Jesus answered him, "Unless I wash you, you have no part with me." None of the others resisted.

"Do you understand what I have done for you?" he asked them when he was finished. "You call me 'Teacher' and 'Lord,' and rightly so, for that is what I am. Now that I, your Lord and Teacher, have washed your feet, you also should wash one another's feet. I have set you an example that you should do as I have done for you. No servant is greater than his master, nor is a messenger greater than the one who sent him. Now that you know these things, you will be blessed if you do them."

After that, Jesus took his seat at the center table and surrounded himself with The Twelve, the inner group of men Jesus often took and taught apart from the multitudes. Jesus' family and friends sat at the outer tables. Mary and Martha had arranged the food on the tables, then sat down with Jesus' mother and sister.

The meal progressed with small conversations at each table, until a ripple of murmuring broke out. Jesus had announced that someone there would betray him, which caused no small commotion among them.

"Is it I, Lord?" Mary heard someone ask. "Surely you don't mean me?" said another. Looks of alarm spread across the room like wildfire.

Jesus answered their concerned questions. "It is one of The Twelve here with me at the table." Then he began to administer the bread and wine to his friends.

After Jesus distributed the bread, he blessed it and said, "Take and eat. This is my body, which is given for you. Do this in remembrance of me." Then he took the cup and gave thanks for it, and, passing it to John said, "Drink from it, all of you. For this is my blood of the new covenant, which is shed for many for the forgiveness of sins."

The bread and the cup went around the entire room, and they all ate and drank in obedient reverence. While she was sipping from the cup, Mary's wary glance had caught Judas quietly excusing himself from the table.

After they had all eaten and taken the sacraments Jesus passed around, a song began somewhere. Every guest joined in until the whole room was singing to the God of Abraham, Isaac and Jacob, claiming Him as their own. Accompanying the song, a fresh zeal swept through the room.

When dinner was over, Jesus asked The Twelve to accompany him to the garden to pray. The women agreed to stay and clean up, and the rest of the men returned to Bethany for the night. Jesus kissed his mother on the way out the door, and Mary had noticed the passionate way she clung to him. She also noticed pain and grief on Jesus' face, hiding behind the smile he flashed her as he left.

That had been hours ago, and the foreboding she felt had only grown stronger. She looked around at the others, unnerved by the sudden awareness of their silence. All of the women seemed stooped beneath an invisible burden and cloaked in the same darkness that Mary felt weighing her down. The work was largely finished, but the women had abandoned what was left and stood wringing their hands, unaware of the world around them.

Suddenly, Mary heard a low rumbling sound. As she listened, it grew stealthily louder until the other women recognized it too. Exchanging horrified looks, they rushed to the door and peered out into the blackness of night.

"Look, there." Martha pointed toward the garden. Their eyes followed her hand up to see pinpricks of light on the horizon, which steadily grew bigger and brighter as the sound increased rapidly. Mary could discern anger and the sound of chains, but the madness did not unfold until it passed right in front of her face. Even then, her mind struggled to receive the message her eyes conveyed. A detachment of soldiers rushed past her, shouting, jeering and angrily jerking along a bloody, bound man. Jesus.

Chapter 28

Mary's hand flew to her mouth to muffle a cry. She turned to Jesus' mother, whose piercing scream kept Mary from her own self-indulging. The older Mary sank to the floor inside the doorway and moaned in helpless agony. Mary gently fell on her as if to cover her from the onslaught of emotions being poured out among the women.

The shouts of the mob dragging Jesus quieted as they charged down the road, but the cries of the women filled in the vacancy left in their wake.

Peter burst suddenly out of the darkness. "I need a cloak!" he yelled urgently.

Someone produced one from somewhere, and Peter ran off again. Seconds later, he returned with John, who was wearing the garment Peter had procured.

"They're taking him to the Sanhedrin," he said excitedly.

"But it's the middle of the night!" Martha exclaimed.

Peter began to say more but was cut off by a quiet, heart-wrenching plea. "I must go to him."

It was Jesus' mother.

"Mother, no. You must not," Peter rebuked her.

John stepped forward and helped her to her feet. "Can't you hear her heart-cry?" he asked compassionately. Gently, John assured her, "Let me go first, to find out where they've taken him. I will come back for you."

Jesus' mother nodded, then slid back into the room.

Mary Magdalene grasped John's hand. "Come back for us, John. Please!"

John nodded his head, then he and Peter disappeared into the night. Huddling together in the front room of the house, the women did their best to comfort one another as they mourned their last sight of Jesus.

"My Jesus," his mother agonized. "My son!"

Enfolding her mother in her arms, Ruth cooed through her own tears. "God will take care of him, Mother. God is with him."

After several hours, which felt like an eternity, Mary heard a knock at the door. Her exhaustion fled as she jumped up to open it. It was Peter. Crying profusely and mumbling incoherently, he stumbled past Mary into the house.

"What happened?" she asked with alarm. Shaking him vigorously, she asked again, "Peter, what is it?"

The other women watched spellbound, waiting for Peter to answer.

"I've – I cannot say it … I've … I denied knowing my Lord," Peter gushed in anguish. He held his head in his hands and wept profusely.

A cold sweat overwhelmed Mary as she thought of how Peter must have felt. The deep pain and regret of knowing what he'd done.

"Peter! What's happening to Jesus?" Martha asked forcefully.

Just then, the door burst open and there stood John. Sweat was running down his face and he was breathing heavily as if he had run the entire length of Jerusalem. He bent over, took great gulps of air then straightened and saw

Peter. John hurried to him and placed a hand on his heaving shoulders. "Brother," he said, "do not lose heart." Turning to the others, he said soberly, "We must go."

Without question, all but Peter followed him out into the street. By this time, the sun was sitting on the edge of the horizon. Mary looked toward the bright hues of morning and let the light kiss her face. She inhaled peace, as she always had from the dawn.

John led them to the governor's palace, where a large mob had already gathered. Mary strained her neck to see above the crowd, and soon her eyes found Jesus. She was shocked by the sight of him.

His hands were still bound. His hair was matted to his head with blood, his face badly beaten. His garments were torn, smattered with blood and hung loosely on his defeated and weak body.

Mary was pulled forward by the panic of Jesus' mother, who was determined to be nearest her son. As she pushed through the angry cluster, she could see large spots on his head and face that were oozing blood, places where his hair had been viciously torn from his head. There were great gashes on his face and neck. Mary resisted her mind's attempts to recreate the scenarios that might have caused them.

Surging forward, the crowd shouted obscenities as soon as Pilate approached the railing of his palace porch. He put his hand up in the air to indicate silence.

"Why am I being awakened so early in the morning to such a raucous? What is it now, Jews?" He spit this last word with disgust.

Caiaphas, the chief priest, stepped forward so that everyone could see him. "We have brought this man to you to be sentenced to death. He defies our laws and has been caught blaspheming. According to our law, he must die."

Turning toward the crowd, Caiaphas encouraged their enraged grievances, to which the mob replied with an awful eruption.

Pilate looked at Jesus, then back at the throng. He gestured for his soldiers to lead Jesus off the porch into his palace. The tumult grew deafening, hurtling curses and threats at Jesus' back.

Mary covered her ears with her hands, trying to drown them out. Her heart went out at the sight of Jesus' mother, who watched the porch fervently, tears streaming down her face. Her lips quivered under the mask of her hands. She looked so small. So weak and needy.

Reaching out, Mary pulled the older woman close to her heart, coddling her like an infant. She knew no other way of comforting her brokenness.

Finally, Pilate appeared on the porch again. "I have questioned him and find no basis for execution."

Caiaphas interrupted him, "That man has traveled all over Judea causing an uproar and teaching strange things to the people. He has come all the way from Galilee and now has even covered all of Jerusalem with his teachings. He's a heretic!"

"So he is a Galilean?" Pilate asked. "Take him to Herod!"

The soldiers brought Jesus out and thrust him toward Caiaphas, whose own guards dragged him away in the direction of Herod's palace. The people followed like a flock of sheep, bleating behind their shepherd all the way across town. Caiaphas could not have been more pleased.

Some of the Pharisees stirred the crowd into a fury after the soldiers disappeared into Herod's palace with Jesus. John pushed his way toward the front, followed closely by the women. Pressed together, they watched expectantly for Jesus to reappear.

A short eternity later, he did reappear and was dragged off in the direction of Pilate's palace by a red-faced Caiaphas. He had been wrapped in a royal purple robe. The same purple that now covered Mary's hair and shoulders. A wreath of thorns bit into the flesh of his forehead. Blood was streaming down his face and into his hair.

Mary rushed with the crowd, helping Jesus' mother along so they would not lose sight of her son.

"Why have you brought him back to me?" Pilate asked angrily when they arrived. "I found no basis to charge him, and neither has Herod. I will flog him and let him go."

He turned to give the order to his men, but Caiaphas screeched hatefully, "No! You must crucify him! We have a law, and according to that law, he must die, for he claims to be the son of God!"

"Blasphemy!" The righteous mob cried out.

The color drained from Pilate's face. He quickly turned and walked indoors, gesturing for Jesus to be led behind him. Several minutes passed, the voice of the crowd sinking lower and lower before dying out. They were all silent, anxiously waiting for Pilate to return.

Returning to his porch, Pilate sat down and, leaning forward with his elbow on his knee, he rubbed his chin thoughtfully. "It is customary for me to release a prisoner this time of year. Shall I release this Jesus back to you?"

A murderous "No!" emitted from the assembly.

"Why not?!" Pilate screamed in frustration.

"Release Barabbas!" Caiaphas yelled, motioning for the crowd to take up the chant. "Release Barabbas!"

Pilate's shoulders fell as the throng took up the cry for him to release a murderer. "What shall I do with Jesus, then?" he bellowed. Mary could hear panic in his voice.

"Crucify him!" Caiaphas screamed. "Crucify him!"

The flock followed their shepherd in demanding that Jesus be crucified. The disciples, the men and women who loved Jesus, looked around at the angry, violent crowd and wept. Mary held Jesus' mother tightly as she shook with emotion. Her sobs pierced Mary, reminding her of the sword of God piercing this fragile mother of Christ.

Pilate ordered Jesus some water, then had a basin brought before him. "You brought this man to me saying he incites the people and claims to be a king. I find no basis for charges against him."

Pointing an angry finger at the tense crowd, he spit out, "You insist again and again that I pronounce judgment against him and have him crucified. I am washing my hands of this. I will not be considered guilty of this man's blood."

Submerging his hands in the basin, Pilate scooped water onto his arms to symbolize his cleansed conscience.

"Let his blood be on us!" a woman cried. "On us and our children! Crucify him!"

"Let his blood be on us," echoed the rest. "Crucify him!" Their bloodlust became deafening. "Crucify him!"

Mary watched as the soldiers led Jesus back into the palace. The thick swarm eventually quieted, then dissipated some as time slowly passed. Jesus had not been led back out to them. Mary stood frozen to the spot, still clutching Jesus' mother, comforting her in her overwhelming pain.

"Where have they taken him?" his mother croaked hoarsely.

"Into the palace," John answered. "If we stay near Caiaphas, we will not lose him."

Mary silently praised this wise suggestion. She was beginning to despair herself, but there was truth in what John said. Caiaphas would not miss anything, so neither would they.

Chapter 29

When Jesus was finally brought out again, Mary shuddered. He was red. His entire body was covered in blood. His flesh was torn to shreds. His face, shoulders, arms and legs bore the marks of a brutal lashing. The soldiers kicked him down the steps of the porch, laughing at his uncoordinated efforts to stand again.

John rushed to him and helped him stand.

"Hey, you!" a soldier yelled, cracking a whip toward John. "Back up. He can stand on his own. Otherwise, how might he carry this?" The soldier heaved a cross toward Jesus, which barely missed his head. It landed hard next to him.

The women gasped. The soldiers hoisted the cross across Jesus' ragged flesh. He slowly turned to find comfort in carrying it, and Mary saw his back. The skin no longer covered his muscles and bone. She clenched her teeth to keep from crying out as she watched the rough wood dig into the open wound.

"Agh!" Jesus groaned.

Fresh tears ran down Mary's cheeks. Her heart was torn at the sight of him. Her savior. In such excruciating pain.

Jesus staggered slowly and with much effort, in the direction the soldiers prodded him. Two other men were walking ahead of him, carrying similar crosses. The whip cracked continuously overhead, often finding a sliver of unadulterated flesh and mutilating it. More often biting into muscle and cutting bone.

Jesus was so weak. How he continued to walk, Mary could not fathom. Finally, he began to falter. His mother broke away and ran to him.

"My son," she whispered desperately.

Jesus met her eyes with silent pleas before John stooped and pulled her away from him.

A soldier ran back and kicked Jesus forcefully. He fell sideways, falling across his cross. With no energy left to get up or even cry out, Jesus laid there, panting helplessly.

"You!" the soldier yelled, pointing at a man among the spectators lining the road.

The man hesitantly stepped forward. The soldier commanded, "Pick him up, and his cross. You will help him."

The stranger bent down and gently lifted a languishing Jesus back to his feet. Soon, the man was covered in Jesus' blood. Picking up the cross, he placed one side of it carefully on Jesus' shoulders, then maneuvered himself under the other side until the weight of it rested more on him than on Christ. Limping slowly, they did their best to catch up to the other prisoners and escape the cracking whip.

Mary could hear Jesus breathing with great effort as the procession left the city and wound its way up a nearby hill called Golgotha. While most of the horde chattered in hysterical jubilation, John and the women walked somberly under a mantle of misery and despair. They wept. They clung to each other, watching helplessly as the soldiers laid Jesus upon his cross.

Mary's nails bit into her hands as the soldier's mercilessly drove thick spikes into the heels of Jesus' hands. His mother choked on her anguish as they placed his feet on a block of wood and hammered them into the base of the cross. Jesus groaned in unutterable torment.

The soldiers carelessly fitted the cross into the ground and raised it to hover over their heads. A cheer went up as Jesus was hoisted into the air. He was unrecognizable even to those who knew him. His body was mangled and his flesh so torn, if they had not been with him from the beginning, they would none have known it was he on the cross.

"Father, forgive them. They don't know what they're doing," Jesus sputtered, with much obvious exertion.

Mary fastened her eyes to him, watching every painful, labored breath he took. Several times, he attempted to cough, then jolted from the pain it caused him.

The soldiers jeered and mocked him. Standing with their arms crossed haughtily, the Pharisees gave their approval to the excruciation. Caiaphas mocked loudly, "He said he was the son of God. Humph! Let him come down now and save himself!"

The crowd chuckled.

"He said he would rebuild the temple in three days? That would be a miracle!" The people howled at the absurdity.

"He can't even get himself off the cross. Miracle worker, come down from there now!" Caiaphas continued mocking Jesus, to the delight of those around him.

Mary kept her eyes on Christ. Several of the other women surrounded his mother, their voices raised in a discordant wail. They were sincerely agonized over his death. Mary pressed her hand over her mouth to hold in the guttural cries that expressed her anguish. Her eyes were riveted to his pain.

"Oh! Oh! Perhaps in a couple days he can raise himself from the dead!" Caiaphas sneered.

The throng roared. The mocking and jeering went on and on. The soldiers bartered for his garments, occasionally giving attention to the dying men, occasionally to the rowdy crew.

Several agonizing hours passed this way. Suddenly, the sky went black and a gentle breeze began to blow. Panic swept through everyone.

"What is happening?"

"Darkness in the middle of the day?"

The centurion hurried to Jesus with a wet sponge. With obvious effort, Jesus turned his head away and refused to drink it.

Someone lit a torch, and by that light, Mary watched the face of her savior contorted by the suffering of death. She watched his chest rise and fall haphazardly. She could hear his teeth grinding amid the rough staccato of his breathing.

She breathed deeply for him, wishing she could help him. She wrapped her purple shawl tighter as the wind grew colder from the darkness. Her eyes never left the flickering figure of Jesus.

Several agonizing hours passed before his voice rang out. "Eloi, eloi! Lema sabachthani!"

Mary's blood ran cold. Her spirit had heard his heart-cry. *"My God, my God! Why have you forsaken me?"*

She watched Jesus struggle for one last breath. In a barely audible voice he declared, "It ... is ... finished," then he hung limp. At last, his agony was past.

As soon as Jesus took his last breath, the earth began to shake violently. Terror filled the people atop Golgotha. A thunderous cracking exploded from the earth around them and they were thrown to the ground by the severity of a sudden earthquake.

Mary fell to the ground near the bloody feet of Jesus. The precious feet she had anointed and kissed. A man fell into her, his eyes wide with terror. It was the centurion who had presided over the crucifixion. His face was ashen.

Looking up at the body of Jesus, he said in horror, "Surely he was the Messiah!" Falling prostrate at Jesus' feet, he poured out his sorrowful repentance as the earth broke apart around them.

Mary lay next to him, her face in the dirt at Jesus' feet until the shaking ceased. Shortly after, the soldiers began to break the legs of the other two men. The criminals screamed in excruciating pain. The soldiers' humor was gone. They simply sought to discharge their duties so they could go home.

One approached Jesus, and Mary cried out. "No! He's already dead. Don't!" She stumbled forward to plead with the man, but the centurion came to his feet and boomed, "No." Thrusting a spear into Jesus' side, the soldier sneered. "Let me make sure he's dead."

Mary groaned and turned her head away. Blood and water burst forth from the puncture and fell on the soldier holding the spear. He spit in disgust and wiped his face with his hand. He looked again at the body of Jesus, and Mary saw a physical change come across his face. Dropping the spear, the soldier looked again at his hands, then fell to his knees and covered his face, this time trembling and sobbing.

The crowd slowly trickled down the hill and disappeared behind the gate of the city. The other women stood grieving at a distance, leaving Mary alone at the foot of the cross.

She stared at Jesus, numb. He told her he would guide her in all things, but his lifeless body hanging on the cross told her nothing. She had left everything to follow him, and this was where he led her. To his death. To the brutality of humanity. The very thing she was running from in the first place. He had abandoned her and left her hopeless, and yet she clung to him.

Mary waited. She didn't know what else to do. She didn't know where to go. She didn't know how to leave him. He was her hope. Her source of peace. Her source of joy and happiness. On whom else could she rely? Mary wiped away the river of tears that flowed from the fresh wound in her heart. Her heart was being crushed. She was perplexed and in despair, aching for him.

At dusk, two men came up the hill and began to pry the nails away from the cross and lower Jesus.

"Where are you taking him?" Mary cried out in distress as she watched them wrap his body.

"Come and see," one of them said to her. They carried Jesus' body gently between them as they made their way to a nearby tomb.

Sitting with Jesus' mother across from the entrance, they watched the men place Jesus inside the tomb and with much effort, roll a very large stone in front of the opening. The light of hope that had grown dimmer throughout the day was extinguished by the finality of the stone being set in place. Jesus was dead.

Chapter 30

Pure adrenaline pushed Mary past the limit of exhaustion. Jesus had been placed in the tomb without ceremony. The women were frantic. Within days, he would be unapproachable. They had already lost one, since the next morning was Sabbath. But if they were prepared, they could get to the tomb early the morning after and anoint his body, giving him proper burial. He was not, after all, a criminal. Spices and herbs were gathered and worked into an olive oil base, then stored in Mary's own alabaster vessel.

The Sabbath was intolerable. Most found refuge in sleeping, but Mary could not sleep. She thought of Jesus' lifeless body, alone in a stranger's tomb. She thought of his smile and the way he had made her feel. The way he had awakened her and liberated her. She thought about late night conversations they had had, and the way he made it feel safe to be herself. The many expressions on his face she had grown to adore.

Every wonderful thing she had ever had in life now lay in a tomb. First her mother, and now Jesus. Loss was such an excruciating, unbearable thing. Mary cradled herself and cried until she had no more tears to shed.

There was no meal that day. There was no conversation. There was hardly any life at all. There were just hapless, hollow people so inwardly grieving they had forgotten themselves.

When darkness fell, a stirring began among them. Tomorrow became the focal point of all hope. Tomorrow they would go to the tomb. Tomorrow they would see his body. Tomorrow, they would grieve together. Tomorrow, tomorrow, tomorrow. The thought of tomorrow helped them remember life again. It was waiting for them, tomorrow.

Mary awoke as usual before the sun. She was instantly full of inexpressible joy and anticipation. Tomorrow had come at last. Without giving it any thought, she reached over and shook Salome.

"Wake up!" she whispered excitedly. "It's time."

Salome sat up quickly, rubbed her eyes and said, "It's still dark, Mary."

"I can't wait, Salome. We must go now."

Salome woke Mary, the mother of James and John, and the three of them quietly stole away with the jar of perfumed oil. Mary led the way to the tomb.

Just as they were topping the hill before it, Mary asked, "Who will roll away the stone?" Then she looked, and dropped the jar in surprise. The stone had already been moved! It was no longer in front of the opening. It had been rolled to the side.

Mary was frightened. She grabbed Salome's wrist, frozen in place by dread and anxiety.

I will rise, Mary.

Racing toward the open tomb, Mary thrust her head through the opening. The sun crested the horizon, shining into the tomb. It was empty.

The women ran quickly, their oil forgotten. Salome and Mary, James' mother, ran back to wake the other women. Mary Magdalene ran to find John.

"They've taken him!" Mary screamed into the doorway of the place the men had stayed.

Peter sat up, dazed and confused. "Wha-"

"They've taken his body," Mary sobbed. "They've taken Jesus out of the tomb and we don't know where they put him!"

Peter bolted for the door, but John was ahead of him. When Peter and Mary finally caught up to him at the tomb, he was standing in the opening, gaping at the sight.

Peter rushed past him into the tomb. John followed. Mary stood near the tomb crying profusely.

She never saw the men leave. She was so wrapped up in her own grief, she didn't see anything. When she could finally stand to, she leaned into the tomb to see it again. The emptiness where Jesus should have been.

To her surprise, there were two men sitting in the place she knew Jesus' body had been. They were dressed simply, in white robes, and they seemed to emanate the light that illuminated the tomb.

"Woman, why are you crying," one of them asked her. "You are looking for Jesus the Nazarene?"

"Yes! Where has he gone? Why have they taken him? Where is my Lord?" Mary cried out passionately.

"Why do you seek the living among the dead?"

Mary was speechless. Their presence, their greeting ... none of it made sense to her.

Mary wiped her face with her shawl. "They've taken my Lord away. And I don't know where they have put him." Her anguish consumed her again, and she bent over under the weight of it as sobs wracked her body.

"He is not here," the other man said. "He is risen."

Mary turned away from the men to hide her suffering. She had heard, but not understood.

Another man approached Mary, although she did not notice. "Woman, why are you crying? Who is it you are looking for," he asked gently.

Straightening to face him and failing to maintain a semblance of composure, Mary begged, "Sir, if you have carried him away, tell me where you have put him and I will get him." The desperate plea was heart-wrenching.

"Mary."

Mary's stomach dropped at the sound of his voice. Her heart leapt up into her throat. "Jesus," she cried as she rushed to him and fell at his feet.

"Do not hold on to me," Jesus cautioned. "I have not yet ascended to my Father. Go to my brothers instead, and tell them to meet me in Galilee. Tell Peter, Mary, that I will see him in Galilee. Tell them I am ascending to my Father and your Father, to my God and yours."

Mary nodded her head wildly, still shocked by the sight of him. When Jesus finished speaking, she turned and ran back toward Jerusalem as fast as she could. She burst into the room where they had all gathered, both the men and the women. "I have seen him!" she exclaimed. "I have seen the Lord!"

"You're mad, woman!" Peter rebuked her harshly.

Levi rushed to her and shook her violently. "Stop it, Mary. You cannot say these things!"

"I have seen him!" she said with defiance. "Just as sure as you are standing there, I have seen Jesus."

"No you haven't. You are out of your mind!" Peter yelled vehemently.

"Peter! Peter!" Mary rushed to Peter and said, "He told me to tell you to go to Galilee. He will meet you there."

Peter looked at her suspiciously. "Please believe me!" she pleaded. "He said to tell you that he is ascending to his Father. To our Father. To our God."

"Shut her up!" Peter screamed miserably before rushing out the door.

"Mary, my dear," came a soft, hoarse voice. It was Jesus' mother. She reached out for Mary and drew her into her arms.

Mary burst into tears. "I'm sorry, Mother. I'm so sorry … I did see him. I did see him."

"Shhhh," the older women cooed. "We are all worn out with grief. Come rest, my child."

Mary allowed herself to sink comfortably to the floor, and Jesus' mother cradled her head in her lap and ran her fingers through her hair until Mary cried herself to sleep.

Chapter 31

Mary awoke to shouting. She was disoriented from exhaustion, and it took a few moments for her to even remember where she was and put the argument she was hearing into context. Then the nightmare returned. Jesus had been killed. The memories flooded her mind again.

"I cannot take this!" Peter scowled. A fury swept over him, then a heart-wrenching sadness. He sank to the floor moaning and finally releasing the anguished cries tucked inside himself.

"What is it?" Mary whispered to the women around her. Salome leaned in and answered, "These two men claim to have seen Jesus today too."

Mary clumsily rushed to them. "Tell me. Please tell me. How did it happen? What did he say?"

She forgot all expected propriety. She was so desperate to be validated. She knew she had seen him!

"We weren't far from here," the taller man began. "We were walking along the road to Emmaus when a man approached us. We were talking about the ... the crucifixion, and he wanted to know every detail. So we told him about Jesus. Then this man started telling *us* about the scriptures, about the prophecies concerning the Messiah. When we reached Emmaus, he was going to go on but we invited him to dine with us first. When we sat down to eat, he broke the bread and began to give thanks. That's when we both realized ... It was Jesus."

"It was not Jesus!" Peter screamed amid sobs. "Jesus is dead!"

Thomas stood and moved toward the men. He leaned in close and through clenched teeth said, "Unless I see the nail marks in his hands and put my fingers where the nails were, and put my hand into his side, I will not believe."

Suddenly, Jesus appeared behind him. "Peace be with you," he said gently. Every head turned toward him. No one moved.

"Put your finger here," he said to Thomas, holding out his hands. "Reach out your hand and put it into my side. Stop doubting and believe."

"My Lord and my God," Thomas choked out in awe.

"Because you have seen, you have believed. Blessed are those who have not seen, yet have believed."

Jesus then addressed the others. "Peter, John, Levi ... you did not believe? Don't you remember what I told you? Everything must be fulfilled about me in the Law of Moses, the Prophets and the Psalms. I told you the Messiah will suffer and rise from the dead on the third day."

Peter stood shakily. He reached out and grabbed hold of Jesus. His eyes overflowed with tears as he embraced his friend. He groaned loudly, pouring out his torment and repentance. Jesus held tightly to him while he cried.

"I forgive you, Peter," Jesus whispered softly.

Still holding a grieving Peter, Jesus turned to the rest of them and spoke the words that drew them all to him at the first. "Friends, won't you follow me?"

Jesus led his disciples, both men and women out into the streets and toward the Mount of Olives. Mary pressed forward to be near him. He turned and smiled at her. "Mary, you were so faithful. Thank you for telling the others."

Mary smiled, but could not find the words to respond. Gratitude flooded her heart.

Jesus stopped, lifted up his hands and began to speak to them all loudly. "All authority in heaven and on earth has been given to me. Therefore, go into all nations and make disciples, baptizing them in the name of the father, and of the son, and of the Holy Spirit, teaching them to obey everything I have commanded you. And surely I am with you always, even to the very end of the age."

Everyone watched in amazement as Jesus' feet left the ground and he rose into the air. Gasps and shouts of surprise accompanied his ascension. Hands followed him upward, as did shouts of exclamation and praise.

Long after he ascended completely, they all stood staring into the skies. Mary was full of expectation, though she could not express its focal point. What was she expecting? For him to come back?

Remembering herself, Mary panicked. "Wait!" she screamed, ignoring the reactions around her. "Wait!" she cried out again, falling to her knees in despair. Jesus forgot to tell her who she was!

A familiar peace descended on her at that moment and Mary heard his voice in her spirit. *"I paid the price, Mary. You are mine."*

Epilogue

"This way, Anna." Mary steered her granddaughter down the well-worn path she remembered from so long ago. "It's just over that ridge," she reassured the girl.

Anna walked slowly, steadying her grandmother's wobbly gait. Mary paid little attention to the road in front of her. Her eyes wandered over the mountainous terrain stretching for miles in every direction around them. She wasn't sure how returning here would make her feel. This place held so many sorrowful memories. Would the memories of Jesus' first coming here overrule the bad ones?

It seemed like another lifetime altogether that she had lived here, desperately far from town and tucked away in between the mountain and the sea.

"Do you remember this, Nana?" Anna asked curiously.

"My dear, I remember all of it," Mary said dreamily. "It was here that he found me. In my darkest hour. I lived in that tiny little house." She pointed as the house slowly came into view. "Right there," she said.

The house was rundown with age and use, clearly abandoned now. Mary stopped in front of the porch and closed her eyes, remembering her youth: the loneliness, the fear, the pain. And finally, the awakening. She turned her head toward the mountain. Her mountain.

"It was there, my daughter," said Mary, pointing toward the heights, "Up there on that mountain, he rescued me. The moment I heard his voice, my heart laid claim to Christ and I followed him recklessly. I gave everything I had to him."

She stopped talking as if suddenly remembering something. "Come this way," she beckoned Anna as she shuffled around the house to the back yard.

Mary gasped.

"What is it, Nana?" Anna asked in concern.

Tears filled Mary's eyes and her hand flew instinctively to cover her gaping mouth. Rooted firmly in her back yard where the garden had been were two trees. Right where Mary had planted the last two vases of money.

"They are the shoot I have planted, the work of my hands, for the display of my splendor," Jesus whispered softly into her heart. *"One plants, another waters, but God gives the increase."*

Mary smiled to herself. "Look, my love," she said softly to Anna. Spreading her hands out like a child displaying a masterpiece, she explained, "I planted the same flower garden year after year here. Small flowers that easily died out and never returned. It was fruitless," she laughed. "But God planted something bigger and more magnificent in its place. These beautiful trees," she said with wonder. "He does all things well."

A Letter to the Reader

This book is categorically a work of fiction. I took liberty with dialogue, people and events directly from the Bible. With that being said, most of the people depicted in this book were real. They had lives, feelings, sins and victories otherwise not recorded in the Bible. I enjoyed imagining this for you to read.

The Bible says Jesus was tempted in every way, yet was without sin (Hebrews 4:15). It obviously goes without saying that he had a life too. Friendships, heartaches, etc. I wanted you to see that! The purpose was so that he could understand what we go through on a daily basis (Hebrews 2:18). This is what qualifies him to stand before God on our behalf.

You may have noticed a familiar ring to a lot of the dialogue coming from Jesus. His words are mostly either direct scriptures or adaptations of scriptures. These words were things his Holy Spirit spoke to me when the Lord was wooing me. In many ways, this book is my testimony. I hope you found comfort in them.

If you have a relationship with the Lord, I pray this book has strengthened you in it. If you don't know the Lord, I pray you will pursue him. Start with the Gospel of John and see where the Spirit leads you. If you know about Jesus and want to be saved, I encourage you to read Romans. The apostle Paul does such an amazing job of explaining forgiveness and salvation.

Finally, if you are interested in contacting me, please send emails to awakeneddawn@yahoo.com. You are also welcome to my blog, www.awakeneddawn.wordpress.com.

Affectionately in Christ,

Dawn Herbert

Made in the USA
Charleston, SC
28 October 2015